BUMFUZZLED
A tale of oil, sand, & romance

DARYL D HANSEN

Archway Publishing books may be ordered through booksellers or by contacting:

Archway Publishing
1663 Liberty Drive
Bloomington, IN 47403
www.archwaypublishing.com
844-669-3957

Because of the dynamic nature of the Internet, any web addresses or links contained in this book may have changed since publication and may no longer be valid. The views expressed in this work are solely those of the author and do not necessarily reflect the views of the publisher, and the publisher hereby disclaims any responsibility for them.

ISBN: 978-1-6657-3609-1 (sc)
ISBN: 978-1-6657-3610-7 (hc)
ISBN: 978-1-6657-3611-4 (e)

Library of Congress Control Number: 2022923917

Print information available on the last page.

Archway Publishing rev. date: 01/20/2023

Chapter 1 ═══════════════════════

The sun had barely set when I got out of the car, stretching my legs. Other than the small, weedy yard where we parked, the entire area was covered with brush and moss- covered trees. Some of them were wild oaks, I thought, and a few of the big ones had moss that hung down almost to the ground.

The only building was an old, deserted house. The whole place right there at dark, had a creepy look to it. Oh, well, we had been in creepy places before. In fact, we had been in all kinds of places.

The door on this end of the house was standing open. It was kind of like it was inviting me in. There was nothing we could do until morning, so, what the heck, might as well have a look.

I stepped up on the old porch, treading carefully, in case the boards might have rotted enough to fall through, but it felt solid enough, so I went on inside.

It was quite dark inside as there didn't seem to be any windows, or openings of any kind to let light in. Gradually, my eyes began to adjust to the dark.

There seemed to be a sort of glow over at the far side of the room, that brightened somewhat. There seemed to be a man there sitting in a big armchair of some kind. It didn't rock, as I would expect, but seemed to glide back and forth, like it was on ball bearings.

The man, whose skin looked like old, tanned leather, was dressed in black, old-style walking pants that ended just below the knee.

His shirt was red, not a tomato red, but more of an orangy red, almost a rusty color. I didn't know whether to greet him, or to turn and run, the whole thing was so weird.

I hesitated, and he stretched out his arm, pointing at me. "You, Yankee boy. What you doing in my house?"

Just then, Tom walked in. He had one of those big flashlight things, you know, with the six-volt battery, that hangs down under it, and as I watched, he turned it on, flooding the room with light.

I turned back and looked. The man in the red shirt was gone, but the armchair was still there, still moving back and forth, although it was slowing now. It seemed to be coasting to a stop.

I asked Tom, "Did you meet anyone as you came in the door?" He assured me that he did not, so I had hm shine his light all around the four walls.

There was no other exit, and what appeared to be a couple of windows, were all boarded up. "This is a creepy old house" Tom said, "What are you

3

doing in there, anyway? We got to get an early start tomorrow."

We went back outside, where we were greeted by Ernie, "What are you guys doing, going in old houses? I don't go in places like that, unless Sadie is inside."

Ernie was an ex-Navy man, and wherever we went, he was always 'looking for Sadie'. I asked him why he didn't go inside and he said, "No, I don't think Sadie would be in a place like that. It just looks creepy weird."

Anyway, we agreed that we needed an early start tomorrow, so we turned in. I liked to sleep in the back seat of the car, while they each had a bunk, on either side, in the truck.

Sometime during the night, I had a nightmare. The guy in the red shirt was pointing at me, saying, "You, Yankee boy, You good boy? Or you bad boy?" I woke up in a sweat. *What's going on here. I saw that guy once, now he's in my dreams.* I finally got back to sleep, about three in the morning.

We were up before dawn. They had some sort of a coffeemaker in the truck, so I joined them for a cup of coffee and a leftover Danish from whatever the last town was that we passed through.

We worked for Global Seismograph service, and they were liable to send us anywhere. None of us had a real home, so if the boss called, or sent a wire, we would just pack up and go.We had been all over the country, and now, we were someplace down south.

I didn't pay any attention to the names of the places we went to.Tom was the crew chief, and he took care of the details.

While we were on our second cup of coffee, I asked Tom. "You didn't see that guy in the old house last night?"

"What guy?"

"The guy in the armchair." "What armchair?"

I decided to put it out of my mind. It was just some sort of a nightmare.

Anyway, we had work to do. We laid out a grid, and every so many steps, I would dig a whole, using an old posthole digger. Then Ernie would plant the charge and wire it into the line. Tom was making a rough map of the locations, and when we had enough charges planted, I would hide behind the truck, while they set it off. Usually all it did was go 'bang' and throw a little mud.

So, by noon, we had three runs made, three little explosions.I didn't think anyone would notice, but suddenly this girl appeared. She just came walking out of the trees. She seemed to be quite upset. "This is private property. Why are you guys trespassing?"

I assured her that we were supposed to be here, she didn't believe me, so I went and got the file from the truck, and showed her the lease agreement. She looked it over. "Well, I guess this just one more thing that Granpa has done without telling me."

She turned on her heel and vanished back into the trees. I was a bit disappointed, because she was the cutest thing I had seen in a coon's age. So, back to work. We finished out that day and the next day, and we had done the whole area that Tom had laid out. Of course, we had no idea of the results. It was all recorded-on charts by the seismograph equipment in the truck, and we would send the charts and graphs in when we got back in the nearest town that had delivery service.

It was nearly dark, and I was just strolling around the area. Actually, I was hoping to see that girl again, but no luck there.

Instead, I saw, just over at the edge of the trees, the guy in the red shirt and black pants. He looked the same, except that I seemed to see, nestled down in his dark, fuzzy hair, some sort of headpiece, not metal, but made of some sort of very dark wood. He pointed a finger at me and said, "Hey, Yankee boy, I decide I like you."

I said, "Well, I'm glad, I guess." He seemed to ignore me, but then, he said, pointing down, "No oil here. Oil over there." I looked to see where he was pointing. It was over at the very edge of land, where a little peninsula of dirt and grass stuck out in into the swamp.

When I looked back, he was gone. I walked over to see where he had pointed. It was only about a block from our last grid. How could it be any different? Yet, the message from the guy seemed so powerful. I had an overwhelming urge to check it out.

I walked back to the truck and told Tom. "I wonder if we might do one more line in the morning, before we leave."

"I guess we could. We have plenty of time, and the lease actually covers more ground."

I slept really well that night. No nightmares, and I was up early. While we had coffee, Tom was telling Ernie. He wants to run a test over by that swamp. Seems to think there's oil there."

"He's not fooling me. I seen him talking to that gal the other day. He thinks he's found his Sadie."

Of course, I protested, and they just laughed about it, but they set, and let me run another line. To get the whole length of it, I even had to wade out into the swamp water about ten feet.

I just pushed the charge down in the mud and pushed some more mud over on top of it. I had it wired ahead of time, and when they set it off, there was quite a loud whoosh of water and mud in the air. Anyway, we had done it, and they were packing up the truck when that girl came out of the trees.

She just stood there looking at me, with a questioning look on her face. Just to make conversation, I said. "How's your grandpa doing today?"

"Not good. He seems to be getting worse by the day. Can't remember anything, and some days he can barely get out of bed."

"I'm sorry to hear that. What is the roblem?"

"Mostly just old age, I guess. Anyway, thanks for asking. Nobody else has."

"You don't have any relatives, then?"

"Nope, just me and Grandpa. It used to be a big family, but now, we're the only ones left." "Yeah. That's the way it goes. I had a big family too, when I was a kid, but I was a lot younger than the rest of them, and now, I'm the only one left."

She looked so sad about the whole thing, I didn't know quite what to say, so I pulled out my wallet and took out one of the company cards I kept there but seldom used. "My names Chris. We won't know the results of the tests here for some time, and I might not get back here, but if you send a letter to this company address, then I will write back to you with the results."

"Okay, I might do that. My name is Jill. I might just send you a letter, you know. Like a pen pal. I always wanted to do that."

"That would be good. I wish I could talk to you more, but the guys are waiting for me." As I walked back to the truck, I turned and looked back. She gave me a little wave and disappeared back into the trees, Of course, Ernie had to say it. "Now, I know he's found his Sadie."

I didn't argue with him. There was an empty spot inside, knowing that I would probably never see her again.

For a guy who had been an only child, raised on a farm with no sisters, this was a hard thing to swallow. Even all through school, I never had a serious girlfriend, and certainly not one who had such an effect on me.

I had the fleeting impression that I had just met the

love of my life, and I had only spoken a few words to her, but what else could I do?

Tom and Ernie got in the seismograph truck and pulled out.

Reluctantly, I started the car and followed.

Chapter 2

They sent us up to Colorado next. So, a couple of days later we were somewhere on what Tom called, the Western Slope of the Rockies.

I didn't have a clue, as usual. Wherever the truck went, I just followed along behind, in the car. We had radios in our vehicles, so if I felt sleepy, and woke up to find them gone, I could just get on the radio, and call Tom and he would give me directions.

As it happened, I was right behind them that morning, as they turned off the highway. We crossed a bridge over a little river and passed a grassy area, with big shade trees, that looked like a nice place for a picnic.

There was not much after that. Just some old buildings on both sides of the street, and some of them were boarded up. On the right, there was an old hotel, but it looked abandoned.

The only sign of life seemed to be at the far end of the street, where a big building with a sign that said **General Store** had an open sign, and a small white building on the left with a sign saying **Antl**ers Bar also had an open sign.

Ernie headed over to check out the bar, while Tom and I went inside the General Store. It was sort of dim inside, but it looked like the kind of place that had just about everything. I saw some racks with work clothes, and some counters with groceries.

A man appeared out of the back. In the dim light, it was hard to tell exactly how old he was, but he was, maybe, five and a half feet tall, with one of those green aprons that had a loop around the neck and a couple strings you tied behind the back. "How can I help you fellas today?" Tom said, "We just stopped in to pick up a few supplies."

"I could cut you off a couple prime steaks. Only take a minute." He pointed over to the other wall, where there was a display case. Like the meat counter in a deli.

"No, thanks, we don't have time to do any cooking. Got work to do." Tom picked up a loaf of bread and a package of sliced cheese.

The man said, "You really ought to have something more than that." He went over to the meat counter and brought back a package of lunchmeat, wrapped in white butcher paper. "Just fresh sliced this morning."

Soon Tom was picking up a jar of pickles and some mustard and a bottle of ketchup. He was piling it all up, and I was already starting to get hungry.

Finally, we piled it on a counter, which was dominated by one of those old-fashioned brass cash registers. First, he added up all the items on an old fashioned adding machine, then he entered that total in the cash register, and cranked the handle on the side. The drawer flew open, and he gave us a total.

Tom asked him if he took credit cards, and the guy just grinned, so we dug around in our pockets and came up with enough. He threw the money in the drawer and closed it. "Paper bags okay?" While he was bagging up our supplies, he asked where we were headed on a fine day like this. Tom told him we were headed up to someplace called the Little Flattops, to do a survey.

He laughed out loud then. "There ain't no way to get up there. Even a horse or a mule couldn't get up there anymore."

Tom dug the little topo map out of his pocket, that showed an X in the middle of a big flat area. They moved some stuff to make room to spread it out on the counter, and the grocer showed him a faint line along the side of what seemed like some sort of mesa.

"This was an old logging road, from back when they were cutting timber up there, back before the big beetle kill, but it has fallen shut. Big rocks on the road."

"Well, the surveyor has already been there."

"Well, he must have walked in. No other way to get there."

"But our boss said we are supposed to check it out and have a test drill outfit come in and drill a test hole."

"Sorry, but the only way you are going to get a truck up there is if it sprouts wings."

Tom was plumb disgusted, and then Ernie came in, saying, "I asked the bartender if Sadie had been there. He growled at me and told me he wasn't running an information center. I could either buy a beer, or get out, so I left."

It was pretty obvious that we were not going to get any help in this town, so we gathered up our paper bags full of supplies and left. We followed the grocers' instructions, however, going through town, and taking a little one lane paved road that tended to bear left for a while. There was one place on a rise, where we stopped.

We could actually see the line of the road going up the side of the flat-topped mountain in the distance.

Then the road seemed to bear to the right, until it came to a three-way junction. We went left, and the road ran uphill for several miles.

Finally, we saw an open flat place, where we could park the truck. There was a faint trail, leading in the right direction. So, we parked the truck there, and all got in the car, which had four-wheel drive. It turned out that the faint track only led to a small lake, so people must have gone that far to fish. After that, we went by guess and by golly, looking down first at a dead forest that had been devastated by a little bug that drilled holes in the bark, releasing all the sap, this killing the trees.

We were still doing okay, looking down into a small lake but then, just around the next corner, the road was blocked by huge boulders.

I had to back up quite a ways, before I could find a place to turn around.

When we got back to where the truck was parked, I thought we might as well pack it in, but Tom was determined.

"Leave the truck here. Maybe we can find a way, in a different town."

So, we drove back down the hill, about ten miles, to where there was a fork in the road.

"Take the left fork this time"

Another five miles or so, and we came to a little hamlet, even smaller than the first one, but it appeared to be a railroad center of some kind. There was a man crossing the road, so I stopped while Tom got out and talked to him. When he got back in, he said,

"We're in luck. There is a man by the name of Dutch Viele, who has a bulldozer."

Fine, but he lived in the first place past the fork in the road. So, I turned around again and drove back the five miles. We finally found the driveway into Dutch Viele's place, and he was willing to do a bulldozer job for us for a fair price.

But he had to walk the bulldozer up there, ten miles, and it did not have a high gear. So, we spent most of the afternoon making sandwiches, in the shade of a couple aspen trees.

When he finally showed up, we got in the car and followed him in, at what seemed like a snail's pace.

Once we got to the blockage, though, Dutch proved himself an able bulldozer operator, pushing those big rocks over the side, and we could hear them crashing on the rocks far below.

When he pushed the last rock over the edge, we were jubilant. Of course, Dutch didn't take credit cards, so Tom got his information and wrote it down in his logbook. They would send him a check. "No problem. Glad I could help out."

As he drove back down the mountain, Tom was on the radio. He got headquarters and they told him that there was a drill rig nearby, and it would be there in the morning.

Everybody was happy and excited. That morning, it had seemed impossible. Now, it seemed, another day and we could be on our way elsewhere. Not that it was not a nice place, out the top of the little Flattops weas kind of like a sheep pasture. No trees, and only short grass stretching in every direction.

So it was, that I was standing there, right next to the stake, beginning to get dark, when the man in the rust- colored shirt appeared, only for a few seconds.

He pointed down, and said, "No oil here."

Before I could protest, he disappeared. It did not surprise me next morning, when the drill rig had only been working for about an hour, and they heard the hiss of gas, and smelled it, coming up out of the drill hole.

The crew worked swiftly, pulling out their drill pipe. They had to get it closed off quickly. If it caught fire, there would be no way to put it out, and they would be in trouble for starting a fire in the wilderness.

They quickly mixed cement, plugging the hole, and left with just a pipe sticking out of the ground to mark the spot.

Nothing we could do but watch the drill rig drive away. All that work and a whole day wasted and we still had to get our act together.

Pick up our maps and our tools, and get back in the car. We still had to get back to where we had left the truck.

Then we had to go looking for a place to eat, and we found it in the town that had a hotel to feed the men who worked on the railroad, in the railroad center.

There was some question whether they would feed us, as we did not work for the railroad, but the cook, a nice lady by name of Vivian. intervened, saying that she still had stew in the pot

"Too bad" Tom said. " It's a really good gas well, but you can't haul it to town in a bucket, and it would be too far to run a pipeline."

Chapter 3 ═══════════════════

They sent us up to Montana next. Not just to Montana, but almost all the way through it. When I saw the sign that said 'Custers Last Stand', I stopped for a while, wandering among the little markers that indicated where sone of his men fell in battle; testimony to the foolishness of the yellow-haired idiot, whose lack of common sense, led them into destruction and death

Anyway, who was I to judge? I never led a small calvary up against an Indian nation with 5000 mounted warriors, but in my younger days, I had done a lot of stupid things, and making bad decisions that had cost me most of my rightful inheritance.

I sat there in the shade of a tree and brooded about

it for a while, but that didn't do any good. Thinking about the past only made me feel bad. I had no one to complain to, and nobody cared what I felt or thought anyway, so I just got a cool bottle of water out of the cooler and got back in the car.

The truck was somewhere ahead of me, but there was only this one road across the trackless landscape. Big Sky Country, they called it, but I might have had a different term for it, *Big Empty country, maybe.*

We drove another half a day, without seeing any sign of a town. Occasionally I might glimpse a farmstead on the other side of a wheat field, where the ripe grain undulated, like waves in the wind. Finally, the radio came to life. "Turnoff ahead. We will wait for you on the corner." *Great, another corner with no signpost. Another dusty road to nowhere.*

Right on. Two tracks with some wispy grass growing in the middle. Miles of dodging potholes and rocks. We finally ended up on some sort of a flat place, like a bench in the middle of nowhere. Not much different from the surrounding territory. It was late in the day, and there was no shade tree, so we just sat on the running board, on the shady side of the truck, while we ate our sandwiches. Tom was the one of us who really liked to eat, and he was bemoaning the fact that this was the last of the lunchmeat and cheese that the grocer had sold us. "So good. Might have to stop in, if we ever get back that way again."

We were all in agreement, but Ernie pointed out that it was not likely. They never sent us to the same place twice. Then the conversation turned to the question we always had. Why did the company geologist pick this place to look for oil?

You might tend to think of oil as being found in a low place, like that swamp down south, but here we were on this flat place that was higher than anything we could see in any direction.

Tom had been to college, and he usually had

answers for our questions, but he couldn't really explain it. "It has to do with anticlines and rock faults deep in the earth, but sometimes, I think the guy is just playing a hunch."

'Well, he seems to be right about one time out of ten," I pointed out. "I guess that's all the company cares about."

Ernie had started out on a farm in Nebraska, but he said he had not been interested in farming, so he went to a vocational school for a while. The only thing there that really interested him was the basic electronics course.

"By then," he said, "The war in the Pacific was starting to heat up, and a friend of mine suggested that we should go sign up.

He said we were bound to get drafted anyway. Probably end up in the infantry. So, he talked me into enlisting in the Navy. That was okay, but it was on my record that I had taken an electronics course. So, they gave me a two-week refresher course, and assigned me to a tin can, as Electronics Mate.

Tom was interested. "How did that work out?" "Not well. That ship didn't want to go to war, and we had all kinds of problems, The second day out, it just quit dead in the water. Everybody agreed that it was an electrical problem. I was supposed to fix it and I didn't have a clue. It took me two days to find the short in a wire, and then the crew was all mad at me when the ship started, because they really didn't want to go to war, either." Ernie was a good storyteller, and he had everybody laughing, but I said we needed to get an early start in the morning, So I said good night, and went to bed in the back seat of the car.

We usually averaged three runs in half a day. Tom had it drawn out on his chart that, since the space was roughly a rectangle, It would take two runs across and six down, so it was possible that we might be able to finish in two days if everything worked right. It did not.

We had some charges that did not detonate. "Could be a bad wire, or a bad detonator" Ernie said. The little detonators were shipped in a separate box, and Ernie inserted them, just before each run. That was the dangerous part of the job.

Anyway, we had to do some of them over, and then we hit some hardpan; ground that was almost as hard as rock, and I had to use a pick.

It was a struggle to get a hole deep enough for the charge, and it was hot and sweaty work. The sun was blazing down and there was no shade to be found anywhere except under the truck, and it was some kind of fox grass, with little stickers in it. It took us three days instead of two, and we were all about tuckered out.

The only good news was that Tom got a message on the radio that when we finished here, we would be going back to headquarters in Denver. That usually meant a few days of R and R, and we liked forward to it eagerly. We finally finished, at the end of the third day. I was going for a walk, because the cool of the evening was the only nice part of the day. There were some butterflies fluttering past. Most of them were the brown Monarch variety. I had read someplace that they wintered in Mexico, so I was sympathetic. They were even further from home than I was.

Suddenly I was aware of another presence there. It's hard to explain, but I knew, even before I saw him, that the little man in the rusty red shirt was there. He didn't say anything; just motioned for me to follow him. We walked over to the very edge of the flat area, where we could look down into an adjoining valley with a little creek on this side, and an open area, like a little park, with a single scraggly tree.

He spoke then. "See, Yankee boy. Oil not up here. Oil down there." I took a closer look, and when I turned back, he was gone.

I thought about it a lot that night. I didn't understand this connection I had with this apparition, or whatever it was, but when he spoke to me, it just felt like the message was burned into my brain.

So, the next morning, as we were having our morning cup of coffee, I asked Tom. "Would you mind terribly if I asked to run one more line before we leave?"

He looked doubtful, but he walked with me over to the edge, where we could look down.

"I guess we could, but we don't have a permit for that area."

"Look around" I said, "there is not a soul anywhere to be seen. Who's going to know? It probably won't amount to anything anyway, and we can always get a permit, after the fact and nobody would notice."

He finally agreed, and Ernie, as usual, just went along with it. It took us a while to find a way to get the truck down there, but the creek was shallow, with a rock bottom. We laid out one line and got the usual location chart and the graph to go with it.

It took an extra half a day, but for some reason, I had a good feeling about it, as we pulled out and headed for Denver.

As I drove along, I thought a lot about the events of the last few days. I did not understand any of it, this connection with some sort of ethereal spirit, who seemed to be taking control of my life in some weird way.

For some reason, I felt that my hum-drum existence was now out of my control. I could only hope it would somehow get better, because even though I had a good job, and clothes on my back, and food in my mouth, my personal life was a mess.

I had no home, no family, and no friends, and although I yearned for a girlfriend, there had never been anyone that even came close.

I had all kinds of hopes and dreams, with no way to expect that any of them might someday come true.

I felt lost and alone, the lost cause of all the lost causes in the world.

Chapter 4

Using his trusty road atlas and GPS, Tom found the quickest route out of Montana. We made Sheridan, Wyoming about dark, and from there it was fast going on I-25. We only stopped a couple times for gas and coffee.

We made Denver early in the morning before the rush-hour traffic. The company maintained an old run-down boarding house near the edge of town, as Global had crews out all over the country, and any of us might be called in at any time for training or re-assignment. I was dead tired, but I managed to open the trunk and drag out my duffel bag, which had all my clothes in it, all needing a wash.

The boarding house was managed by a couple, who reminded me of the old tale *Jack Sprat could eat no fat, his wife could eat no lean.* He was like a bean pole, with a face that was dominated by ears and nose. She was very round but always with a nice smile. I checked in with him, but I dropped my duffel bag at her feet, handing her a couple of twenties. She smiled and assured me the laundry would be taken care of, in short order. I knew there was a laundromat just down the street, but I was so tired, I could barely stay awake until I reached my room. I promptly fell in bed and slept all the rest of that day. Sometime before dark, I roused myself from slumber long enough to go to supper at the diner down the street. It was good to sit down to a real meal once again.

But I was still tired, so I went back to bed and slept through the night. No nightmares. I had already decided to put the guy in the rustyred shirt out of my mind.

The next morning, I was finally caught up on sleep. I had been doing this for quite a while, going short on sleep and catching up. It seemed to be part of my natural rhythm.

It was a beautiful morning, and I was sitting on a bench, in a public park, next to a little lake, watching some ducks that were swimming around in circles. I saw the reason why, when a family strolled by; the kids throwing out some old bread crusts, which the ducks consumed as fast as it hit the water.

It was nice, the family and all, and I was thinking about it, wondering if I would ever have a family like that. Not likely, but it didn't hurt to dream about it.

My reverie was interrupted by the Global messenger boy on his bicycle. "Been looking all over for you. There is a meeting at the head office in an hour." He handed me an envelope, got back on his bicycle, and pedaled away.

What? My dream of having a quiet week off was

suddenly blown to shreds. My car was parked back at the boarding house, so I threw the envelope in the back seat and forgot about it as I drove to the Global office, which was on a street a few blocks west.

The truck was already in the parking lot, and I parked next to it. Tom and Ernie were already in the lobby, waiting for me. "What's going on?"

"Don't have a clue." Tom said, "The messenger got us both out of the sack this morning. I was hoping to sleep in."

Even Ernie looked a bit sleepy. "I suppose they are going to send us out to somewhere in Never, never, land. I bet we will be on the road again before the end of the day."

We were all guessing where we might be sent this time. Our conjectures were interrupted, however, by the receptionist, who said. "Mr. Ferguson will see you now."

That got my attention. Mr. Ferguson was the boss,

not the *big* boss, but close. We followed the receptionist down the hall to one of those fancy glassed-in offices and I knew something was up. As long as I had worked for Global, I had never been here before.

She indicated that we should sit in the three chairs provided, and we sat. In a few minutes a man in a suit came in through the other door and sat down on the other side of the desk. I assumed that this was Mr. Ferguson, although he didn't say so. "He said, "Good morning, and we all responded, "Good morning."

Then it was all quiet for a while, as he studied various papers in the two files in front of him. Finally, he looked up. "It seems that Mr. Goodrich has chosen you for a special assignment."

He pushed that file to the side. "However, we have a few details we need to take care of first."

I had a feeling of foreboding. This couldn't be good. I was prepared for the worst, but not for what he said next.

"It seems that you fellows have achieved some re-markable results on two out of the three last missions."

Suddenly, it hit me. This was the two times when the weird guy said, "oil over there."

Mr. Ferguson went on to say, "Very good results indeed, but a certain anomaly in each of those, should we say? In neither case did the successful find match the original layout chart."

We all figured we were in trouble now, and Tom and Ernie turned to look at me. They didn't point a finger, exactly, but they wanted to make it clear that it was not their fault.

Mr. Ferguson studied the file for a few moments. "Our geologists in the lab have studied both of these, and they are in agreement. The board met this morn-ing, and it has been decided to send in a drilling rig to both of these sites."

"The only problem is that, since the site does not match the original chart, we need a man on the ground, to make sure they don't drill in the wrong spot. A mistake in location, at that point, could be very costly, don't you agree?" All three of us nodded in agreement.

"All right, we have two locations, and the drill rig is scheduled to arrive at each of them tomorrow. So, who goes where? One is in Montana and the other one is in Louisiana."

There was a stunned silence for a moment, then I spoke up. "If Tom and Ernie took a company car, and took turns driving, they could make it to the Montana site on time. Easy."

Mr. Ferguson looked right at me. "All right, do you think you can be there on time?"

I assured him that I could, even if it meant driving all night.

Mr. Ferguson stood up, and we followed suit. We thought we were done, but he said. "Don't forget you have to be back here in three days. Your flight out is already booked, and the arrangements made for your next mission."

Suddenly I realized what I had done. I would have to drive to Louisiana and back in three days. I should have told him that I needed another driver to help out. Too late now, as we were being shown out the front door. ``In the parking lot, Ernie and Tom both said, "See you in three days."

"Sure you will" I answered, although I wasn't sure at all.

No time to go back to the boarding house for my laundry. I headed south. I had to drive through Denver first. Thank heavens it was not rush hour, no traffic tie-ups, so I buzzed on through without a hitch. Same with Colorado Springs.

I stopped in Pueblo to gas up and got a couple burgers and fries from a drive-up. Past there, there was little traffic, until I cleared the pass, and turned onto the highway that stretched to the southeast across the barren landscape, the road that would take me to my destination.

I drove all night, no problem. I was well rested, and it didn't bother me. I only stopped a couple times for gas and coffee on the good road through Oklahoma, and by morning I was in Louisiana.

I had a little trouble finding my way to the site, as I had just been following the truck the first time. I got out my well-worn copy of the road atlas and traced it out with my finger.

Finally, I drove down the faint excuse for a road and pulled off to park in the weed-grown yard next to the old, deserted house.

Now, I stopped to check my time. It was afternoon, and I had to be back at the office the day after tomorrow. No time to waste. I walked back to the place where the land protruded out into the swamp.

I was hoping to see the girl again, but no luck there. I knew she lived somewhere back in the trees, but I had no idea where, and I didn't have time to go looking for her, so I went back to the car.

I had a box in the trunk, with a couple charges in it, and a couple detonators, packed in sawdust, along with a small roll of the red and white wire. I went back to the swamp, and wired up a charge, just pushing it down with my foot. I set it off, using the six volt battery from my flashlight. It made a satisfying **Whoomp** when I set it off. Then I moved over about ten feet and did it again. This time it was even better, with a lot of grass and mud flying in the air.

It must have been louder, too, because this time the girl came running out of the trees. She saw me and stopped, with a surprised look on her face.

"What are you doing here?"

"Long story" I said, "I wish I had time to tell you, but I don't." I looked back and I could already see the drill rig coming down the road. She had no idea what was going on, and I didn't have time to explain it. She just looked at me, and to try to make conversation, I said, "how's Grandpa?"

"He died. A couple of the neighbors helped with the burial."

"I guess this property belongs to you now?" "Oh, yes, Grandpa saw to that, before he began to lose his memory."

I had to ask. "So, what are you going to do now?"

"I don't know. The old house is falling apart, and the roof leaks. I can't fix any of it, so I guess I will have to go somewhere and get a job."

The drill rig was really close now. I could see the silhouettes of two men through the windshield.

Something came over me then, and I took out my wallet, and removed the blank check that I kept there for emergencies. I wrote out a check and signed it and handed it to her. I said, "consider this a loan. Just be sure to write to that company address that I gave you on that card, so they will know where you end up.

They will need to send you checks for your royalties."
She had a puzzled look on her face. She said, "Thanks,
Chris", folded up the check and put it in her pocket.
She didn't even look at it.

The drill rig was here now, and the driver was getting out of the cab, and I had to point out to him the
proper place to drill.

"Oh" he said, "I thought it was back here," "No,
it's over there," and we walked over to the edge of the
swamp. I showed him the proper spot to drill. I could
see Jill, looking up at that huge drilling rig. She had
probably never seen anything like it.

He pushed a little stake into the ground, right
where I pointed, and when I looked back, the girl was
gone, vanished into the trees.

I didn't have time to go look for her, as I was already a bit behind schedule, so I told the driver. "Just
do me a favor, okay? While you're drilling, if a girl

comes out of the trees, just offer her a ride to the nearest town, okay?"

He assured me he would, and I got back in the car and headed for Denver.

Chapter 5

I was just coming back into Denver, when the radio came alive. "You're a little late, Buddy. Better hustle your but up here, pronto. Mr. Ferguson is getting anxious."

Fine, I was doing the best I could, but it was still morning, and I was catching the last of the rush hour traffic. Getting through Denver was no picnic, lots of stop and go, so when I pulled into the parking lot at Global, Ernie and Tom, were both standing beside the truck, waiting for me.

I started to make excuses, but tom said. "It doesn't matter. We already had the meeting. Ferguson was telling us how fortunate we are, because Mr., Goodrich had picked us for this special mission."

"What special mission?"

"Don't have a clue. He just handed me these two envelopes, and the receptionist showed us out the door. Before she closed it, she said, "You better clean out your vehicles. A company car will take you to the airport." Tom showed me the two envelopes. One had written on it, in big black letters. ***Do not open until you are ready to board the plane.***

The other one had written in big red letters, ***Confidential, to be handed over to Mr McGruderr at the Global office in Norfolk.***

We stood there a few minutes trying to figure it out, but then we saw the company car coming to pick us up, so Tom said we had better get busy and clean our vehicles out.

It was then that I found the envelope. It had fallen

off the back seat and was partially hidden under the seat in front of it. I put it in my pocket.

There wasn't much else I had to take with me. My sunglasses off the dash and a little spare change. I asked the driver if he would please stop at the boarding house and pick up my laundry.

My duffel bag was sitting in the corner next to the desk. I didn't see Jack Spratt, or his wife, but it didn't matter, as there were guys like us in and out all the time.

It was on the way to the airport that we started to talk about where we might be headed. None of us was sure, but Ernie said, "When I joined the Navy, we shipped out of San Diego, to go to war in the Pacific, but I think those going to the Atlantic shipped out of Norfolk."

"Well, I find that hard to believe." All those years I worked for Global, they never shipped anybody overseas. The driver dropped us off at the airport door marked, **Departures,** The attendant on duty took our luggage, which consisted of a duffel bag each.

A man in a Global uniform met us at the door, saying that we were right on time, and he would be delighted to show us the way to the proper gate.

Now, we were thirty minutes early, so we sat down, and Tom opened the envelope, Nothing in there but three boarding passes to Norfolk.

It was only a few minutes before we heard the announcement. **Now boarding Flight 317 to Norfolk. We will board passes numbered A to F first.** That was us, so we showed our boarding passes, and walked the covered ramp to the plane.

The Stewardess greeted us, and we followed her to the left. I was overjoyed to see that we were in first class. I had flown a few times before, but never in first class. It had those layback comfortable seats, so, while the Stewardess was taking Tom's and Ernie's orders for drinks, I just lay back and went to sleep.

Three days of driving and I was worn out. I didn't care if we were going to Timbuctoo, or the Canary Islands. This was my chance to get caught up on sleep.

I Don't know how long I slept, but I'm sure it was most of the trip. When I woke, I saw that Tom and Ernie were asleep, both of their chairs in a laid-back position. There were only two other people in first class, and they were both staring out the windows, like they were trying to see something below.

It was then that I remembered the envelope in my pocket, the one that Global messenger had delivered to me a few days previously.me in care of Global. I opened it and read it quickly. The girl was not big on wording, but she was keeping good on her promise to be a pen pal.

Dear Chris,

Weather fine. Grandpa is not so good. Wish you were here.

It was signed, *Jill*, with a big flourish. It might not be much as her first attempt at a pen pal letter, but it certainly caught my attention. I could hardly believe it. Wish you were here, she said. Almost an invitation to get to know her better, maybe to start a relationship.

No wonder, she looked at me as though she was expecting something more. I should have given her a hug, or maybe a kiss on the cheek, anything, but instead I just prattled on, asking about her grandpa and what she was going to and instead I had given her a check.

Well, it was too late now. The die was cast, and I would probably not see her again, or not at least for a few years. As it turned out, it would be over two years, but I had no way of knowing that at the time.

The sign came on, saying "**Fasten your seat belts,** with a ittlle 'Ding' that woke Tom and Ernie, and we prepared for a landing, with no idea of where we were going, or why.

In the terminal, we were greeted by a man with a nice blue jacket on. On the pocket was the emblem of the Global organization. "I will be your guide while you are here. Just come with me."

We piled into a car with the Global emblem on the side and he drove us a short distance to a very nice hotel. He let us out there. As he was about to leave, Tom asked him, "What about this package?"

"Hang onto it. You must deliver it personally. It is very important. Do not let it out of your sight."

I had a question, "What about our duffel bags?" "Don't worry about them, they are being delivered, as we speak. If you need anything at all, for tonight, just charge it to Global. We have an account here." That was all I needed to hear. There was a nice restaurant, so we really lived it up, ordering our favorite things from the menu.

There was a sort of mini mall in the hotel, with a clothing store, so I bought some new socks and underwear, charging my purchases to Global.

Then, the room, with a bed so soft. I sort of floated down into it. Another chance to catch up on sleep. I didn't care. Let tomorrow take care of itself. I was happy.

I would not have been so happy, if I had known what the future had in store for the three of us.

Chapter 6

Our driver found us at breakfast. We were all well rested, as well as well fed. The driver, however, seemed extremely anxious to be on our way, although trying not to be obvious about it.

The only thing he said was to ask Tom if he had the envelope in his possession. Tom did, resting on the floor beside his chair. Soon we agreed that we had our fill of breakfast, and as we got up to leave, I asked the driver if I should go back to the room, as I had some dirty laundry there.

"Forget it" he said, "you will be issued new clothes before you leave. Right now, we have a busy day ahead of us. No time to waste."

So, basically, I was starting out with just my sunglasses, my billfold, and the letter in my pocket.

He drove us, in the Global car, down to the dock area. A couple times, looking down empty streets, we had glimpses of the ocean, and the docks, with a couple ships tied up. Not one of those big cruise ships. This appeared to be a work area.

He parked in an empty space next to what looked like an old warehouse, with wooden steps leading up to an unused loading dock. I was beginning to get a bit nervous, as it looked like some scene from a gangster movie.

When we entered, we got a big surprise. Inside it was very modern, with bright lights and glassed-in cubicles. It looked like any modern office building. The driver led us down the aisle to the last office, and introduced us to Mr. McGillicudy, a middle aged man with wispy hair, thick glasses and an intelligent look.

We were barely introduced, when he said, "I believe

you have something for me." Tom handed over the envelope, and the man ripped it open and dumped the contents on the desk.

He then proceeded to arrange them into little piles on his desk. Finally, he said. "Good. They are all here."

Now, we, the three of us, had not a clue what was going on. Our sudden departure from Denver, and the plane ride to Norfolk; it all seemed like some weird weekend at Comey Island, or something. Finally, Tom spoke up. "I think we could use an explanation." Ernie and I were nodding our heads in agreement.

"But of course." He said. "You see here we have three passports, three visas, and three tickets for boat passage. That is all we need for now." He shoved the three piles into a drawer and said, "Please follow me."

He opened a door behind him, and there was nothing to do but follow him. There was what appeared to be a big garage that was built all across the back of the building. Mechanics were working on a couple of the cars, with Global markings on the side, but he led us over to the other end of the floor, where a couple of vehicles sat by themselves.

There was something weird about them, and it took a moment to comprehend. The man explained. "You see we have adapted these vehicles for a special purpose. Your old ones were four by fours. These are six by six."

It was a sudden revelation. Why would we need a vehicle that had six-wheel drive? Just the look of the truck and the car, both oversize, and with four wheels in the back instead of two, was enough to make me nervous. I asked him, "Why would we need that many wheels?"

"Oh, my dear boy. It is to help from getting stuck in the sand. Even then it may not be enough." He opened a door in the side of the truck, showing some sort of wire grid things, a whole pile of them. "Sometimes, you will have to use these, as well."

It was then that it registered with Ernie. "Bloody hell, they're sending us to a desert."

"But of course." The man said, "one of the biggest deserts in the world."

"Wait just a darned minute." I said, "I'm not going anyplace until I get an explanation." "Did they not tell you? Mr. Goodrich chose you for this mission. It is a special job, very important, but it must be done in the strictest confidence. You must tell no one; no one at all. Do you understand?"

He went back to showing Tom and Ernie all the other special compartments on the truck. I heard them say something about an extra heavy duty air conditioner, but I was looking at the car. The hood and the trunk were normal, but the car in between had obviously been lengthened, to accommodate the extra wheels.

Also, there was not the usual metal top. Instead, the top was some kind of very heavy canvas, like a convertible top, but there appeared to be no way to let it down.One of the mechanics saw me looking at it, and he came over to help me.

"Fixed this one up special, we did." He had me get into the driver's seat and began to show me. "The gearshift is a bit tricky at first."

He indicated two metal rods coming up out of the floor. "The bigger one is a regular four speed and re-verse, but the shorter one is like a shift that will take it all down by one-third.

That way, you will have grandma gear for the really tough spots. Also, there is a hand throttle here on the dash. Using that, you can leave it run in the lowest gear, while you get out and move the sand mats."

Well, by now, my anxiety was about to get out of the roof, but I figured I better just keep my mouth shut and listen, since it all seemed to be out of my control. Later, there would be times I was glad I did, many times in fact.

Now he was showing me all the features of the canvas top. "You see with all these canvas patches fastened up like this, you can let the wind blow through. This car doesn't have air conditioning like the truck, and this is usually better, anyway. Then, if you get caught in a sandstorm, you just put them all down and close it up,"

He showed me, with all the pieces velcroed and zippered into place. It was as tight and close inside as any car with the windows closed. Maybe tighter.

Then he got out and showed me the trunk. It also had been enlarged. Inside was two of everything. Two white containers for water.

Two red containers for petrol, two spare tires and two jacks.

All on a wooden shelf and underneath that, a couple of sand mats, "In case you happen to get separated from the truck." There was also enough space for supplies, and if I tried really hard, I might be able to cram my duffel bag in, before I closed it.

"Okay I hope that helps. The boss is coming, so I better get back to work."

The boss, it turned out, was Mr. McGillicudy, with Tom and Ernie in tow.

He was telling them that these two vehicles would be going with us on the ship. "But first, you have to have orientation." We followed him into some sort of conference room, where a couple of guys in coats with Global emblems took turns talking about desert survival. They showed us a first aid kit, talking about how to treat things like sunburn and frostbite. We stopped once, when sandwiches and drinks were brought in. Shortly after that, Mr. Mcgillicuddy announced that it was time to go. He handed each of us a passport, a visa, and a ticket for the boat passage. He also gave us a journal, saying that it was a special gift from Mr.

Goodrich, and he would like us to keep a record so that he could read all about it on our return.

We didn't even need a driver. We just walked down to the dock. There was an old, weathered building with a sign that said **Immigration and customs.** We showed him our passports, the customs man asked if we had anything to declare, which was a stupid question as we were totally empty handed. He gave us a little wave, and we walked up the gangplank. Ernie said, "We're probably going to be on this tub for at least five days." I was shown to my cabin, and it had a comfortable bunk, so I didn't care. I had no idea, really, where we were going, or what we might have to do. I decided to put it out of my mind and pretend that I was on vacation. Blissful ignorance. If I had had any idea of what we were getting into, I would have jumped overboard before we left the dock.

Chapter 7

The sign beside the road said *Juliet, Home to 310 happy people.* The drill rig slowed, and Dan said, "We might as well stop here for a bite of supper." Dan was the crew chief and Arnie was his helper.

She had watched them at work for a week, while their crew had drilled down in the swamp. She was fascinated by it all, especially by the man in the tower, who handled the pipe so expertly, each time they added to the string, or the couple times they had pulled it all out to change bits.

"We're going through a layer of real hard rock down there," Dan told her. "That might be a good thing. Sometimes there is oil under it."

She was almost sad when they pulled up the drill stem the last time, and began the process of laying the tower over, ready to travel elsewhere. "We have it spudded in, and the crew will be here next week, to install the pump."

She didn't understand any of that oil talk. She only knew that when they left, she would be left alone again, with no grandpa to care for.

So, when Dan asked her if she would like a ride someplace, she was quick to accept the offer. While they finished preparing the rig for travel, she ran home to collect her belongings, Only a few worn out clothes, and only a few dollars and some odd change in Grandpa's cookie jar. She put the money in her pocket and rolled her belongings up in an old blue tablecloth.

At the last minute, she remembered the check and the card that Chris had given her. *Be sure to write and tell the company where you end up.* He said it was important, so she would do that, for sure.

The truck that carried the drill rig was huge. She needed help to climb up and get in the cab, but it also had a sleeper, so she could sit on the bunk and talk to them, one would drive and then the other.

Then never seemed to need the sleeper anyway. They drove for a couple days, only stopping now and then for coffee. Dan made it clear that he would drop her off anyplace she chose, but nothing felt right to her.

Now, they pulled over at a roadside diner. They were big guys, always hungry, but they always went to the men's restroom and washed up before they ate, so she did the same in the Ladies.

When she came back, a friendly waitress was talking with them, a nice-looking girl, with dark hair and a slight tan. She looked to be about her own age. The two men ordered big meals, but she just ordered a piece of toast, buttered. It was the cheapest thing on the menu, and when the waitress set it on the counter in front of her, she was counting out the change from her pocket. She barely had enough to pay for the toast

The waitress looked her in the eye, and asked, "Things a little tight right now?"

"You might say that. It's all I've got." She looked like she was about ready to cry.

The waitress said, "None of that now. Didn't you read the sign? Juliet is a happy place."

"Well, I guess I should be thankful for something. At least these guys are giving me a ride."

"You heading anyplace special?"

"Nope, they said they would drop me off any place I chose, but I haven't seen a single place that looks like home."

"Really, where is home?"

"Well, it was in a swamp in Louisiana, but Grandpa died."

The waitress thought about that for a few minutes,

then went to refill the coffee cups for Dan and Arnie. They looked like good dependable working men, the kind she liked for customers.

She was chewing her way through her toast when the waitress came back. "So, how did you happen to hitch a ride with those guys?"

"They were drilling a well next to the swamp, and when they folded up the rig, they offered me a ride. I had no family left then and the old house was falling apart, so when they offered me a ride, I just cleaned out the cookie jar and got in the truck."

By now, the waitress had decided that it was all on the level, being very careful, she had enough experience with travelers to know when somebody was running from the law.

She said, "I'm Molly, Welcome to Juliet." She stuck out her hand. She shook it and said, I'm Jill, and I'm happy to be here."

"If you should decide to stay, you see there is a help wanted sign in the window."

Jill looked, she was tempted but she said, "I don't know. I don't have a car and no place to stay."

"I have a little place out back. It's not much, but it has two bedrooms and I'm only using one."

"But I don't know anything about waiting tables."

"Nothing to it. Just hang around this evening and watch me. In the morning you can meet the boss, and we will get you a little uniform like mine."

It was a quick decision, but when Dan and Arnie paid their check, she told them, "I think I will just stay here."

She followed them out to the truck, and Dan handed her belongings down to her, all still wrapped up in a blue tablecloth.

Chapter 8

We were well out to sea by the time I awoke. I didn't know how long I had slept, but, looking out the little porthole, I realized it was daylight, so I must have been asleep all night and part of the next day.

Anyway, I felt well rested, so I decided to venture out. I was in a little hallway, with five doors on each side. As I was to find out later, this was a cargo ship, but they also had ten rooms for passengers who wanted cheap passage across the ocean.

There were no amenities. Nothing fancy like you would expect on a cruise ship. Just this passageway, that ended in what might be loosely called a 'mess hall' with a long table at one side, and small tables and chairs on the other side. It seemed that the coffeepot was always on, and at mealtimes, there would be some food spread out on the table, usually just some lunch-meat and cheese

It would have been a sorry food selection, but once a day, the cook would bake some big loaves of bread, which became my main staple.

At the far end of the mess, was a slanted ladder going up and a similar ladder going down on each side of the room. That made the mess available to the entire crew, no matter which part of the ship they might be stationed on. I took the up ladder and found that I could step out on an open area beside the bridge.

I could look in through the glass, and see the men steering the ship, or I could look out at the vast ocean, which was not blue as I might have expected. No blue sky to reflect, there was always a high overcast of moisture in the air, which seemed to result in a dirty gray look to the water.

My first look at that dreary ocean gave me an uneasy feeling. As far as you could see, in any direction, there were only these little rows of wavetops. We seemed to be crossing them at an angle, and every time, the ship would roll a little one way, and then back the other way.

It gave my stomach a rolling sensation. Every time the ship rolled; my stomach rolled in unison.

I didn't understand about seasickness then. I still had that to look forward to.

I could look forward, out over the deck, which was about a hundred feet long. There were two cargo hold openings in the deck, with a small cargo crane situated between them. One had a big cover on it, made of wood and canvas, and I saw there were four men struggling to fit a similar cover on the other one.

There was a man on each side of this big square thing, and it was obviously very heavy. I watched them as they struggled with it. A couple times, a man slipped, as the ship rolled, and they nearly dropped it, but recovered. I guess they worked at it for a half- hour at least, but they finally got it settled into place, and I saw one of the men, with a big hammer, was nailing it into place.

I watched that sea making those endless waves a while longer, but that rolling was making me increasingly uneasy, so I went back down the ladder way, to find that lunch was spread out on the big table, along with a couple big loaves of fresh-baked bread. I was hungry, and I really tore into it, pulling off hunks of bread, and slathering them with butter, and then layering on lunchmeat and cheese, along with onions and pickles and olives.

A big mistake. A man, freshly on a ship, should eat light, because the more you cram down there, the more there is to come up.

Anyway, after a big meal, I naturally felt like a nap, so I returned to my cabin. It was then that I started writing in my journal. I had some weird idea that if I kept a record of everything that happened to us, I could make a story out of it, and I would present it to Mr. Goodrich when we returned in a couple of months. How naïve.

I got the letter from the girl out of my pocket and used it as a bookmark. I would take it out and read it every day, and it would become my one hope in a sea of despair, in times to come.

Wish you were here, it said, and I would fantasize over that endlessly, imagining different scenarios, where I would return to the swamp and sweep her into my arms and carry her away, like a knight in shining armor. I fell asleep on my bunk, and I guess I slept the afternoon away. I was awakened by a knock on the door. "The captain requests your presence at his table for dinner."

Great, I washed up and proceeded to the mess hall. Tom and Ernie were already there, and greeted me, but they didn't really seem so happy to see me. It dawned on me then. They were blaming me for us being here, because I was the one who said, "let's do a run over there."

The fact that they had proved out was the thing that got the attention of the big boss.

They blamed me, and I blamed the weird guy in the rusty-red shirt, but how could I explain that?

I took a seat, and in a few minutes, the captain appeared. He was a typical stocky seafaring man with grey hair showing under his Captain's cap, and with a white gray, neatly trimmed, beard to match. When he spoke, I caught a strong accent, most likely Swedish or Norwegian, I thought.

He was quite soft-spoken and polite, welcoming us on board his ship. I saw there were other passengers, being seated at the other tables, so it was obviously an honor for us to be invited to his table the first night out.

It was all fine, until a steward brought out some bowls of stew, placing a bowl of what appeared to be a mixture of meat and vegetables, all cooked together in some sort of brown gravy.

The captain folded his napkin neatly and placed it in his lap. We followed suit. He took a big spoonful of the stew and began to chew it with pleasure. I took a big bite. It was delicious, but just then the ship took an unusually big roll, hanging there for a second, before settling back. I heard the captain say, "We might be in for a spell of bad weather." It hit me then, and I got up and ran for the 'up' ladder. I barely made it to the bridge and leaned over the rail before all that food I had been putting down came up so violently that it left me gasping for breath.

I was sick, off and on, most of the night. I gave up on trying to make it up the ladder, only getting as far as the little bathroom. The result was that my whole little compartment started to smell like vomit, which made me feel even worse.

By morning, I had rid myself of every ounce of food that I had taken in the day previously. I managed to drag myself to the mess for a cup of coffee. That made me feel a little better, so I hauled myself up to the bridge, as I wanted to know about the storm. The ship was rolling so violently now, that I had to haul my self-hand over hand up the ladder.

It was a chaotic scene. The wind was blowing water over the bulwarks on the side of the decks, and a wave of water would sweep across the deck. Some of the water would drain out through the scuppers, but then the ship would roll back and then the wave of water would sweep across the other way, only to be added to, as the wind blew another batch of water over the side.

I was beginning to wonder if the ship might sink, but one of the crew, a first mate, I think, saw me hanging over the rail.

"No problem "he said, "It seems a low pressure area has developed into a hurricane, but we have changed course to get around the worst of it. It might take us a bit longer to get there, but we will make it."

Encouraged, I headed back to my room, and I saw that I was not the only one who was seasick. Two of the other passengers were in the mess hall, and they were both carrying buckets. Why didn't I think of that?

I spent most of the day in my bunk, even though there were times the ship rolled so violently that I nearly rolled out onto the floor. It seemed to be getting worse not better, but I was starting to feel better. I could not see anything out of the porthole, nothing but waves of foam and spray washing across the glass, so I decided to make the effort to have another look.

I took the up ladder, holding on tightly, as the ship was rolling so badly now that it was hard to stay upright. When I got out onto the bridge, I saw that one of the other passengers had given up on his bucket. He had tied himself to the rail with some rope, and he looked a bit green around the gills. Looking out, it was much worse than before, there had been some boxes of cargo stored out on the deck. The crew had thrown nets over them, but now the wind was tearing the nets away, and some of the crates were simply sailing away in the wind. Not just the crates.

I saw that one of the cargo hold covers was beginning to tear loose from its moorings. It was flopping up and down, and even above the wind, I could hear the screech of the nails as they were pulled out by the sheer force of the wind.

Now, I was sure we were going to sink, as the whole deck was awash. I could just picture it, the hold cover gone and the water pouring down into the hold.

No place to be, out in this storm, but before I went inside, I untied the rope and helped that guy off the bridge. It was a struggle to get him down the stairs, but I left him in a chair in the mess. It looked like he might survive. I saw there was some bread left on the table. I grabbed a chunk of it. Without any butter on it, or anything, it seemed to make me feel better, and I finally fell asleep.

The next morning, the storm was gone. Just like that, barely a ripple in the water, but my journal entry for that day said "*June 26, Bad cstorm, -sick, sick, SICK.*

Chapter 9

The next morning dawned bright and clear. I could look out the porthole and see the surface of the ocean. It was almost flat, and the ship had very little roll. I washed up, the best I could, and went to the mess. My stomach was not ready for food yet, but there was some juice.

I had a glass of that, and there was some of yesterday's bread, sliced up and grilled.

A slice of that and I was satisfied.

While I was there, the man came in that I had untied from the rail the night before. He was quite effusive with his gratitude. "I felt so bad that I wanted to just end it all right there. Then I became afraid that

I might not die, and the torment might continue. I hate to think what might have happened if you had not come and rescued me. I might not be here today."

"It was no problem, really. I felt just as bad, and I had to get back down the stairs anyway."

He saw what I was having so he selected the same, and we sat down at one of the small tables, while we drank our juice. It turned out that his name was David Lang, and he traveled the world, selling machine parts for a big supply company.

"That's the way it is these days, you know. They want always bigger sales at lower expense, so they send me on the slow boat. I know I could make bigger sales, if they sent me by plane. I could cover more ground, visit my customers, more often, give better service, but try telling that to the home office."

He was a nice guy, probably British in origin, and he liked to talk, which was fine with me. I am usually a better listener myself.

Eventually, it was my turn to speak, and I asked him, "Where are you headed this time?" "Well, I think that all of us on this boat are headed for the same place."

"What place is that?" I said without thinking. "Why, Marrakech, of course. Didn't you know that?"

"No, it seems that, what with being sick and all, I have missed the conversations on our destination." He grinned. He obviously had never met anyone on a ship that didn't know where they were going.

Then, when I admitted to him that I had never heard of such a town, and had no idea what country it was in, he laughed out loud. "Well, Marrakech is the capital of Morocco."

I still had a puzzled look on my face, "well, I didn't do so well in Geography. You know that name sounds sort of familiar, but I can't quite place it."

This just delighted him, no end. "My dear boy,

Morocco is the first country we come to, when we reach the coast of Africa."

"Oh, right" I said. "I guess they did mention something about a big desert.'

He was really enjoying this now. "One of the five biggest deserts in the world, and I suppose you are going out into it."

I admitted that I was a part of a three-man crew, being sent out into that desert.

"Dear me, you are in worse shape than I was when I was tied to the rail. In a hurricane."

He was still laughing when he headed down the hallway to his room. Now, I had something to think about. No wonder Tom and Ernie were upset with me. This was beginning to sound like a suicide mission.

I had read enough books back when I was in school that told what a dangerous place the Sahara Desert could be. There were stories about the heat, the sandstorms, snakes, scorpions, lack of water and numerous other things.

For a minute I thought about turning back, Maybe I could jump ship when we docked, but where would I go?

I finally decided that it didn't matter. Nobody lives forever, anyway, and I had no family, nobody cared. It might be a fun way to go, as good as any. Anyway, I started looking for some way to pass the time. That is when I made a monumental decision. I would pursue the journal keeping idea, but not for the benefit of Mr. Goodrich.

No. I decided to make it a record of my story; the story of everything that happened to me, going back to the day when he first met the weird guy in the rusty-red shirt.

The story that I might want to tell my grandkids someday, assuming that I ever had any, and assuming that I could survive the desert. That was the big question at the moment.

So, I settled down with my journal and began to write. Uppermost in my mind was the nagging question. What had become of the girl? I had left her standing there, at the edge of the swamp, her Grandpa dead, their house in disrepair, with no family and no hope.

He spent most of that day, writing in his journal, but the next day, he got to thinking about the water pouring into the damaged hatch cover, so he decided to go check on their vehicles. From the lunchroom, he took the down stairway this time, and found that he had to go down two flights of stairs. At that point, he could hear the engines working away, even further down, but there was a door leading into the hold.

It didn't take him long to find the two vehicles, parked side by side, and strapped down so they could not move. Fortunately, they were not in the compartment with the damaged hatch cover, but just to pass the time, he checked them out. There were manuals that came with both vehicles, and he set about learning how each and every part of them functioned.

If he was going to be sent off into a desert somewhere, he was determined that he was going to at least know how everything worked. He saw Tom and Ernie several times, but they were playing some sort of a card game with a couple of the other passengers. The sea was fairly smooth and the rest of the trip uneventful. They were set to land in Marrakech in a couple days. He looked forward to it with certain anticipation. He decided that it was best not to complain. More could be achieved, by waiting and by keeping his eyes open. He was resigned now to the fact that they were being sent to one of the most fearsome deserts in the world. Maybe the desert would defeat him, but he was not going to give up without a fight,

Chapter 10

Jill was doing fine. With Molly's guidance, she had met with the owner. He was also breakfast cook, and his name was Dale Rockhill. He assured her that he really did need help. With four waitresses, they could do two shifts, an early shift and a late shift. Two waitresses on each shift would work best for all of them.

So, jill started right in. Molly was soon teaching her how to separate the customers.

The good guys, that liked it when you talked to them; and the other guys, the wolves on the prowl, and the occasional hoodlums that might wander into a roadside diner.

Jill was naturally friendly, with an easygoing

personality. Soon she was pouring coffee and taking orders, putting tips in her apron pocket, just like Molly did. Most of their customers were regulars, who chatted with each other while they ate. They chose the early shift, the breakfast crowd, so they were off work by mid-afternoon.

Since they were sharing the expenses of Molly's little house, they both began to save up a little money, talking about a day when they would go the city on a shopping spree.

So, one afternoon, Jill asked Molly if she had any writing materials. She explained about the guy who had shown up one day, and how he made her promise that she would write to this address on the card he had given her. Let that company, Global, know where she was at.

No problem. Molly had stationery and envelopes and stamps. So, with that one completed, she said, "I also told him that I would send him a pen pal letter"

She was still not sure what to say, but included things like, Working with Molly. And doing okay, and as before, she ended with *Wish you were here.*

She showed it to Molly. "Do you think this is okay?"

"Well, I'm sure it is. Jill, is this guy your boyfriend?"

"Well, I guess he is, in a way. He was so nice to me, and he was the only guy that ever gave me anything."

"Really? What did he give you?"

Jill showed her the check. Molly looked at it and exclaimed, "Jill, this guy must really be in love with you."

"Oh, I don't think so, why?"

"This is a check for ten thousand dollars."

Jill looked puzzled. "I guess that's a lot then. I never had much to do with money, other than Grandpa's little pension check." "Jill, do you know what this means? With this much, you are a rich woman." "But I don't want to be a rich woman. I want to be like everyone else. Besides, it's not like that. He said it was like a loan, until I got some royalty checks. So, you see, it's not my money, really. I'm just keeping it for him. I don't even know what to do with that check."

"Well, I do. I'm going to march you over to the bank and get you set up with an account. Let them worry about what to do with the check."

Molly thought about it all for a moment. "Does this have anything to do with that oil drilling rig you showed up in?"

"I guess so. Dan and Arnie drilled on Grandpa's property for a week. I watched them do it, and Dan said it was done and the pump would be set in a few days. It was a lot of oil talk, and I didn't understand any of it."

"But they completed a well, and you told me your grandpa died. So, who inherited the property?"

"Well, I did. I was his only relative." Molly threw

her hands in the air. "Not only is my roommate rich, but she also owns an oilfield in Louisiana."

"Really, it's not like that. Please don't tell anybody."

"Okay, whatever you say, but first, let's take a walk down to the Bank."

Chapter 11

It was mid-morning when they docked in Marrakech. He stood out on the bridge wing and watched, while the captain maneuvered the ship carefully into place; giving an order to the first mate, who would make adjustments while speaking into the telegraph that carried his words down to the engine room. There was also a tugboat on the outer side pushing them closer to the dock.

Hardly like the days of the old sailing schooners. The only thing that was the same was when they tied up to the dock. They still used big ropes, probably eight inches thick, that the crew threw over the side. A crew on the ground placed them over the stout posts there and winches drew them tightly to the dock. The hatch cover had been removed and he could watch while the crane lifted their vehicles out of the hold and set them on the dock. A gangway was positioned on the side of the ship, but before they had a chance to depart the ship, the captain told them. "Do not leave the dock area yet. Instructions from your company"

When Tom asked why, he told them, "A guide is being sent. You three would not last long in the desert on your own" Very encouraging.

It felt good to be back on solid ground once more. He had enough of that rolling motion to last him for a lifetime, which, as he considered it, might not be very long. At least the dock area looked like any other dock area in the world.

Lots of ships in various sizes were being loaded or unloaded. A short distance away, he could see the top half of one of those big cruise ships over the top of the warehouses. Apparently, this was a port of call for some of those luxury cruises he had read about. People with lots of money to spend and a need to be pampered, probably hundreds of them on that one ship.

Ernie and Tom spotted a dockside pub, gave him a little wave, and went off. Chris had no intention of going off in a strange place by himself, so he settled into the car, with both doors open, letting the slight breeze blow through. It was early in the day, but already you could feel the heat rising, that and the humidity, and he was sweating already.

He sat there for the best part of an hour. He was beginning to feel drowsy when he saw a man come walking across the dock area. A big man, at least six foot – two, with a solid, muscular look.

He was square -jawed and tan, with a crew cut. Reminded him of the woodsman in his little storybook, that single-handedly chopped down the entire forest.

The man strode right up to the car, leaned down to

look inside and introduced himself. Chris got out of the car and shook his hand. He didn't catch the man's entire name but was told, "Everybody calls me Mac."

"Where's the rest of your crew?"

"Over there in the pub. I think Ernie is looking for Sadie."

Mac got in the car. "Might as well drive us over there. No use walking in this heat, when we can ride" He drove over and parked in front of the pub and sat there while Mac went inside. He felt like he was being tested. Good thing he had studied up on it and knew how to start the car.

In about three minutes, Mac came out and got back in the car, telling him, "Let's go"

He saw, in his rear-view mirror, Tom and Ernie come racing out of the pub and running for the truck.

"Teach them to not be lollygaggin' around when there is work to be done"

We drove just around the end of a warehouse and

waited in a shady place. Soon the radio came on. It was Tom. "Wait. We have to figure out how this thing works"

Mac keyed the radio. "if you can't keep up here, how the hell are you going to keep up out in the desert?"

Chris was beginning to get a kick out of this. Mac was wasting no time getting this crew in line. Of course, he was grinning the whole time.

By the time the truck caught up with them, Chris already had the feeling that, just maybe, they might survive the desert experience, after all. Following Mac's directions, he drove through the city, leaving the dock area far behind.

Now, he was seeing the darndest mixture of street traffic. A few old cars and trucks, but mostly bicycles, motorbikes, an occasional rickshaw, a mule or two, and a string of camels. He had to drive slowly to keep from running into something, as there seemed to be no order to the traffic. "Is it always like this?"

"Oh, no, this is a quiet day. Sometimes it's much worse. Just take your time. We have time to kill. We don't go out till Monday"

Chris soon learned that they had a schedule. Go out on Monday, look for oil, come back on Friday. Rest two days. Pick up new orders. Go back out again on Monday.

"It's all just routine. You will get used to it" "You been doing this long?"

"Guiding a seismograph unit? Nope, first time for that, but I been around here for almost twenty years doing one thing and another. It's all about the same when you go out into the desert. Doesn't matter why. Out there, we're all the same, all trying to survive"

Mac indicated that we should turn into a driveway. There was a little road under a row of palm trees. They stopped in a parking lot. The building had an emblem on the front, but it wasn't Global. He asked Mac about it.

"Seems your company entered into some sort of agreement with an African oil company. For some reason, they think there might be oil out here someplace, but their seismograph trucks are all busy, working in an oilfield over by the Great Depression. So, they split the expenses, and if you happen to find oil, they split the profits."

"Well, do you think there is any oil out there?"

"I don't have a clue. I don't know anything about finding oil. That's what you guys are here for"

The truck was pulling in behind them, but as they got out of the car, Chris noticed a man sitting in a little building off to the side, between two small palms. He pointed, and Mac said, "Guard house. Night and day. These vehicles are quite valuable and must be protected at all costs."

This was the first indication that things might be

quite different here. They never had to mount a guard, anywhere they had been, in the States. Mac led them into the building on the right of the one with the emblem on it.

"This is set up by the company, as employee housing." It was very similar to the one in Denver, even to the fact that it seemed to be run by a couple, but the similarity ended there. The couple seemed to be very dark. It was hard to tell, as they wore those Arab type clothes, like sheets wrapped around them and with a sash of a different color, tied around them at the waist. Also, this place had a dining room, and as they entered, a small servant girl was setting out food on a table at the side. Sort of a help yourself arrangement, like that on the ship, but a much greater variety of food. At first glance, there seemed to be a lot of fruit, but there were things there he could not recognize.

The proprietor spoke up. "Sasha will show you to your rooms first. You should wash up, before you come and eat." He spoke perfect English, but with a heavy accent.

The lady said nothing, leading them down a dim hallway that had two doors on each side. As she came to the door, she would open it. As each man looked in, he saw that his duffle bag lying on the bed, with his name stenciled on it.

Chris checked out the bed, not bad, and there was a closet and a little bathroom with a shower. Not very fancy, but serviceable. It appeared that this was to be their home away from home, for a very long time.

Chapter 12

Certain things a man begins to value, when you live and work in a desert environment. Number one for me was the morning shower on the weekends.

There would be many times when I would sit and dream about that shower, during days when my clothes were soaked with sweat, and one of those little 'dust devils' would spring up; a wind out of nowhere, stirring the dust and fine sand into the air. It would stick to us, like the frosting on a cake, and we would all be walking around like mud-stick figures, unable to tell who it was.

It was then that I would dream about the shower,

standing in it with the lukewarm water running down my back. A feeling like no other.

Then there were the weekend breakfasts, a table loaded with goodies; certain kinds of figs and dates that I was partial to, and some little green bananas, picked fresh off a tree. For the main course, often, a thing that looked like a breakfast burrito, but was called a falafel, with lamb and filling inside. A lot of things we ate without having a clue.

It's hard to explain, but after five days out, with only some sort of C-rations to eat, everything fresh took on new importance. Trivial things lost importance. We no longer thought of money as anything of value. In fact, I was unsure of my pay. It was automatically deposited in an account somewhere.

All we needed were bare necessities for survival, and one of the things I valued most was a wool blanket, of all things.

Anyway, we had arrived on a Saturday, and Sunday,

we were free to do whatever we chose, with a couple exceptions. As Mac explained to us that first morning. We could not take the vehicles into town.

Parking was almost nonexistent, and if you did find a place to park, the attendant might charge you five bucks to park, but you might return in an hour, to find the vehicle sitting on blocks: the wheels, the tires, and the attendant gone.

He could sell those wheels for enough to support his family for months. However, we were told that the bus service was very good, and the bus would run every hour, with the bus stop just outside the gate. Of course, Ernie and Tom were anxious to go into town, 'looking for Sadie' but they were cautioned by Mac to be back before evening, as we would be leaving at daybreak the next morning, So it would be necessary to check everything out ahead of time.

Lots to do, the water containers full. Drinking water was the first priority. A man might survive a week without food, but three days without water. The story was that a man who got lost from a caravan, somehow survived five days, but when found, his skin had turned black, and his own relatives did not recognize him.

We also had to be sure our gas tanks and jerry cans were full. To run out of gas a hundred miles from town could be fatal if you were off the beaten track.

Then there were things like food, and the supplies for the truck, the charges, detonators, and the graph paper for the seismograph equipment. Lots of things to think about, and I was glad to see that everyone was taking it all seriously.

We had a big challenge ahead of us, and we would all have to work together to accomplish it. We were supposed to go out and find oil in a part of the desert where there were no proven oil reserves, and it seemed to me that, once again, there were some geologists that were working on nothing more than a hunch. They seemed to wander around randomly, drive a couple strakes in the ground, and draw a rough chart of the locations. Maybe just a few lines drawn on an old topo map.

These would be handed to us, in the office, on a Monday morning, at daybreak, and we were supposed to go out there in a trackless desert and find the location, run some lines, and bring our charts and graphs back by Friday evening.

That may sound easy enough, but there were times when we thought that climbing Mount Everest would be easier.

Breakfast was over, and I was wandering around in the yard, just checking out a few bushes and small palms; plants I had never seen before.

Mac suggested that perhaps I might like to go and visit the downtown area of Marrakech once, just in case I should have to go down there for any reason. We walked out to the end of the lane, and in a few minutes, a blue and tan bus appeared. So far, this seemed like any town, anywhere.

The bus went back in the direction we had come from yesterday; towards the docks, but suddenly turned right onto a wide street, that soon turned into a divided parkway. We were headed, it seemed, right towards the area where that big cruise ship was moored.

Nothing could have prepared me for the scene downtown. There were people everywhere, and everything was in motion. I saw Arab men in their flowing robes and big turbans.

There was a group standing on a corner that looked like Chinese businessmen in dark suits. Soon I realized that there were people here from every country in the world.

There were little curbside cafes, with dark skinned men, cooking over charcoal fires, and I saw people walking down the street, eating something on a stick. Their version of a walking burrito, I guess.

The main street was quite wide, with traffic in both directions, but no place to park. In a few places there were little signs, in several different languages, and one of them said, **Loading zone. Five minute limit.** While I watched, a sedan pulled up, and two ladies got out, wearing fur coats. Imagine.

It was already starting to heat up, maybe in the 90's, but of course, the lady's car was air conditioned, and they disappeared inside a store with a polished marble front. Some kind of a salon. They probably had an appointment to get their nails done or their hair fixed. I had no idea what ladies did these days. A group of men walked by, having a heated discussion. They seemed to be Scandinavian, perhaps Swedes or Danes. There were people here from every country in the world, mostly with the look of tourists, with little cameras in hand, taking snapshots of each other.

And everywhere, there were the kids, most of them around ten years old, handing out brochures. One of them came up to me, saying, "you take, my tour? I like very much you take my tour." I looked at the brochure he handed me. It advertised a three-day camel trip into the desert, with a camp and food.

Mac informed me that there were all kinds of tour companies. Some were on camels and some riding ATVs. They had paths and trails worn into the surrounding areas, but none of them went out into the real desert. They wouldn't last long out there.

"If you ever want to take a tour" he informed me, "the tour to the Atlas Mountains is the best one, but it takes five or six days." He pointed to the east, where the tops of some rather barren looking mountains could be seen, perhaps twenty or thirty miles away.

A group of boys went by on bicycles and then two young girls on motorbikes, and an older lady in a rickshaw, pulled by a little old man. "Best way to get around" was Mac's comment. "Beats a taxi, any day."

The sidewalk was congested now with foot traffic and the boys saying, "Take my tour" were becoming a bit annoying, so we turned off into a side street, one of many in that area.

There were no sidewalks here. People just walked in the street. We passed a kiosk, and I saw the posters advertising the tour to the Atlas Mountains. The skinny little man sitting on a stool inside it, leaned out over the counter, offering me a brochure. I took it and a little further along there was a café with a couple of tables and chairs out front. We took a seat and I read the brochure while Mac ordered us some drinks.

According to the brochure, there were any number of different tours you could take, by car, camel, or motorbike. The least number of days involved was four, but if you wanted the full experience, you could go for ten, with everything provided.

I kind of gasped at the price quoted for that one. Obviously not my thing. The drinks were very good; might have been a little rum in there, and some goat's milk, Mac told me.

When we had finished our drinks, I threw the brochure in a trash barrel, and we went on down the street, just looking in the shop windows. All kinds of souvenirs and junk, all for the tourists, nothing you could actually use.

We turned right at the next corner; the idea being to go around the block and back to Main Street, where we could catch the bus.

This was a back street, with no sidewalks and no shops. I was thinking about other things, I guess, when Mac grabbed my arm. I looked up to see a grey car, that was headed right for me.

Mac jumped into an empty doorway, pulling me in with him. The car missed by less than a foot and sped off before I could get a good look. I only had the impression that there were two men inside, and the license plate with covered wit dirt.

Once I caught my breath, I asked Mac, "Why would anybody want to run over us?"

He just smiled, "You're in Africa now. There are always unseen forces, with opposing views. In this case, I think there may be an opposing oil company that thinks this area belongs to them. Maybe they don't like the idea of you guys searching for oil in their part of the country."

I started to say that we had been told to keep it all confidential, but then the image came to mind of Ernie and Tom, playing cards with a couple of shady-looking characters on the ship.

I suddenly realized that I knew Ernie's life story, pretty much, but I knew nothing at all about Tom. The few times I had tried to talk to him about it, he always seemed to change the subject.

Anyway, I had seen all I wanted downtown, so we

caught the bus back, had a light snack for lunch and took a nap.

As instructed, Ernie and Tom returned before evening, and we worked until dark. Everything had to be checked, the oil in the motor, the gas in the tank, the water in the window washers.

There was a garden hose to fill every water container we could come up with. I had the two white jerry cans in my trunk, but I also scrounged up some used canteens, and a couple of green plastic ones that clipped on my belt.

There was a gas pump over by the trees close to where the man sat in his little guard shack. Nobody else here now, but tomorrow there will be cars here; people coming to work in the office building. I still didn't know the name of the company we were working for.

It was some name I couldn't even pronounce, and anyway, we were still getting paid by Global. At least

I hoped we were. I never actually saw a paycheck, but it didn't matter.

No place to spend money out in the desert. Anyway, I got my car all gassed up, the red jerry cans full of petrol, and went inside where boxes of supplies were stacked up behind the counter; mostly some different sorts of dried foods, kind of like what the infantry lived off of. I crammed as much as I could in every nook and cranny. I barely had room to jam my duffle bag on top, before I closed the trunk.

I would soon learn that a lot of that was unnecessary, and in the following weeks, I would cut a lot of that in half., to make more room for water. Mac spent most of the evening helping those guys in the truck, as there were more things to check there, such as the air conditioning unit, and the graph papers for the seismograph equipment.

The sun was well gone by the time we finished, and

I went off to my room, with a mixture of anticipation and dread about what we would face the next day.

In spite of that, I was tired enough that I had barely fallen into bed, and soon was fast asleep.

Chapter 13

We were awakened by banging on the door, accompanied by a loud "Up. Time for up." The building manager apparently took his wake-up call duties seriously. I managed to roll out of bed and find the light switch in the dark.

I showered and dressed quickly. I would really have liked to linger in the shower for a while, but who wants to be the last one to breakfast on the first morning of a new job?

We gathered in the dining room, the four of us, everyone sleepy eyed, and quiet. We could almost hear each other chew; each lost in our own thoughts. This was the day we would find out if we had what it took to deal with the desert.

The quiet was interrupted by a messenger boy. He started to hand a big manila envelope to Mac, but he waved him off.

"Not me, I'm just the guide. Tom is the crew chief."

Tom opened the envelope and shuffled through a stack of papers.

"Good Lord, what are we supposed to do with all this?"

Mac took a quick look. "All we need, for now, is the top one. Leave the rest of them in the envelope" He quickly explained that the area we were to explore was many miles away. First, we needed to find the area, then look at the charts and maps for specific locations. Our search area was some 50 miles wide by 70 miles long. Bad enough, but it didn't start until we were 45 miles from the city.

As we tried to digest this information, it became

evident that Tom may be crew chief, but Mac was the leader, because he was the only one who had any idea how to go about such an impossible task.

So, as we stumbled out and got in our Tom. He had best get them checked out on desert driving, he told me. I got in the car and followed as we rolled down the lane, and the first faint glimmer of dawn was just beginning to show in the east, as we turned right and headed south for the Sahara.

In the beginning, it was a nice little two-lane paved road, but we had only gone a few miles when it started to deteriorate, the edges breaking off or covered in sand.

As it started to get light, I saw, in the rearview mirror, the gray car following us. No headlights, they were just following my taillights, and I wondered if I should be worried.

But suddenly I had bigger things to worry about.

There was a sign that said, in big red letters: **next 250 miles**

That barely soaked into my consciousness, when I looked down. The road had disappeared. It might still be there, but it was now covered in wind-blown sand, which seemed to be drifting across in front of my headlights, like the first snowflakes in a blizzard.

I soon noticed that the gray car was no longer there. It seems that they had no inclination to tackle the great sand desert, and I began to wonder how in the world we would ever find our way back again. All I could do was follow the truck. It plowed steadily ahead, so Mac must have some idea where we were going.

It was still pretty good going, for a couple hours, as we were running mostly on a packed sand surface, but then we began to see sand dunes on either side, and we began to zig and zag between them, wherever there was a gap. It was very apparent then, that there was no road anywhere, according to the compass on my dashboard, we were just heading in a mostly south direction, sometimes with a little jag to the east.

We were not out there even half a day, and already, if I were on my own, I could not have found my way back to town. Then, the sun became a blazing fire in the sky, and the temperature rose rapidly. I had both a dash thermometer and a clock and by noon, it was already 110 degrees.

That was inside the car, with the windows down and a breeze blowing through. We stopped for a while, taking a break in a large open flat place.

Mac was warning us. "it's good to sweat, but re-member, every pint of water that goes out, has to be replaced by a pint of water going in Drink water often the first couple days. After a while, you will get used to it, and your body will tell you when it needs water"

Another couple hours, and we developed our first problem. The temperature was over 120 degrees and the truck radiator started to heat up. They stopped with steam rolling out under the hood. It turned out that their big air conditioner was run by a big compressor hooked to the motor. It was fine when they were sitting still, but when in gear, the motor developed more heat than the radiator could dissipate.

So, when we were driving, they had to sweat it out with the windows down, just like me. For some reason, that made me feel better. In the desert, it sometimes is the small things that become important.

We were traveling much slower now. More sand dunes, and sometimes we would start down an open lead, only to find it was a dead end, and we would have to backtrack.

Well, 45 miles didn't sound like so much, but we did not find our search area that first day. We camped and Mac told us the first few days would be a learning experience. We had to work out our own routes, and once we did that, there would come a day when we would find our way in and out quite easily.

There did not seem to be any twilight. It was like the sun was there, blazing one minute and then suddenly it would be swallowed up by a sand dune. As darkness set in, the sand gave up its heat rapidly, and the cool of the evening was a nice time to sit out.

We would search around for any dry sticks or gras, or even dry camel dung, anything that would burn. We would scoop out a low place in the sand, get a small fire going, and Mac had some kind of a round metal thing he would fill with water from his canteen. He would set it right in the fire, and once the water got hot, he produced some little teacups, made of some kind of composite, so they wouldn't break if we dropped them, and they wouldn't melt in the heat.

He had a couple tins of tea, and you would just take a pinch or two of tea in your cup, pour some hot water over it, and wait a sec for the leaves to settle.

It soon became the highlight of our day, evening teatime in the Sahara Desert.

Mac pointed at my blue jeans. "You're going to find those a bit too hot."

"Well, I've only got two legs and I am kind of attached to them"

"You're worried about the little things, are you? The sidewinders and the scorpions?" He pointed out his boots. "See, all you need are a good pair of boots like this, tough leather." The boots came up to mid-calf. "Those critters, if you happen to step on one in the dark, will only bite you ankle high, and they can't get their fangs through this thick leather" It was all part of my learning experience. The next time in town, I got a pair of boots, and some over the knee walking shorts like Mac wore.

For now, though, I slept in the car, and if I needed to get up during the night, I turned on my big flashlight and searched the ground in every direction before stepping out.

I could only say that it was a learning experience; finding out what we needed to get when we got back in town.

Not only that; just learning to use the things we had. That would become a series of hardlearned lessons, in the days to come.

That was the big thing in the desert. You learned, or you died.

Chapter 14

The second day I would remember as the biggest learning day of my life. Not a good day. A terrible day, but things learned that would help us through in the future.

It didn't start out so badly. It's rather nice just after first light, still cool, and we started out with confidence. There was a mixture of terrain here. A few sand dunes, and we saw the Sshaped tracks in the sand, left by a sidewinder as he made his way up and over the top. As I soon learned, all the reptiles tended to bed down at night, because it would get quite cool, even sometimes downright cold before morning. There was a snake called a coral snake, that would just dive down under the sand at night. As it warmed up in the morning, it would suddenly pop up out of the sand, with bright rings of red and yellow and black, the most colorful thing in the entire desert. Also, the most poisonous.

Watch for it, but don't get too close. No problem, but in some areas, there were scorpions. In one place, kind of a shady area, I saw a whole family of black ones, some as big as my hand.

Another thing to avoid.

We saw our first evidence of a camel caravan, and Mac explained that we were operating in the territory claimed by the Touregs, a nomadic tribe, that had lived in this vast desert for many years.

They traded different goods, but the most common caravan was one that would start far east of here, near Lake Chad, where there was a huge deposit of salt.

Workers there would dig the salt out in blocks, and it would be packed in big bags, tied to pack saddles on the backs of camels, as much as 300 pounds per animal. There might be as many as fifty camels in the caravan.

It might take a month to reach a destination such as Timbuktu, which lies to the south of us. There was no salt to be had in that area, and Mac pointed out that in a hot area, it was necessary to have some salt, for both people and animals. Otherwise, the water you took in would just run on through. You needed to have a little salt to retain some water in your system, and we had salt tablets in our kit, so we took one, morning and night.

We were doing fine, driving across a big flat, when we saw our first mirage. It looked like a huge lake shimmering in the heat. I could almost swear that I could see palm trees. We were all looking at that mirage and instead of following, I was driving out alongside, although separated by about fifty feet. Now there was apparently some kind of an old ditch, or maybe just a long depression, only about ten feet wide. It had filled in with blow sand, and when we hit it, our wheels just went down into it; *Woomph,* and we were so stuck. The radio came on, with Mac saying. "Shut your motor off quick. Don't spin your wheels"

Too late, I had already spun the wheels once, which just churned the sand and put the car in deeper. Of course, we had those sand mats, but you had to get one end of them under the tire. We had a little shovel in each outfit, so I started to dig.

Now sand, being the loose grained little devil of a thing that it is, will run back down into the hole almost as fast as you can dig it out. I soon had a huge hole there and I still could not get down to the bottom of the tire. So, I took a break while I thought about it. I had two jacks but of course, they would just jack down into the sand.

I finally figured out that if I emptied the trunk, that wooden shelf would be made in two sections. I could take it apart, using some screwdrivers from my tool kit, and place the boards under the rear bumper, and set the jacks on the boards, while I jacked the car up, but then, because of the springs, it still didn't raise the wheels up out of the sand enough, so I had to jack it up with one so I could get the other one under far enough to get it under the frame, then jack that up enough to move one under the axle.

Finally, with a bit more shovel work, I managed to get the ends of the sand mats under the rear wheels, and I got the car backed out of the sand ditch. It only took me about an hour, but it took half of a day, to get the truck out. Even when we got sand mats under it, I had to find a big tow strap in our supplies. Tied to my bumper, I used that to pull, while Tom drove the truck and Mac and Ernie pushed.

A big lesson learned. After that the car took the lead with me driving and Mac in the passenger seat. Several times, during the next couple days, he would holler "Stop" and I would slam on the brakes, in time that only the front wheels were down in the loose sand. Just back out and drive around it. The other problem we had was that we were in an area that had some sparse clumps, of a grassy looking plant, some kind of spinniflex, I think. It looked harmless, but the roots of the plant must have been there for a decade, and the soil around it had baked into a rock-hard substance. If you happened to run a wheel over it, it would send the car bouncing up, and our heads would hit the roof. Good thing it wasn't metal, although the oak supports were almost as hard.

If you only got too close to it, sometimes it would break off, and fly up between the fender and the tire, and that wheel would *clunk* to a sudden stop. Then we had to get the jack out and jack the car up enough to let it fall out.

Altogether, it was a tough day. The only good thing was that we finally found the corner of our search area. It as marked on the map, **Boulder,** and suddenly there it was, a big brownish rock, worn smooth by the blowing sand, bigger than the truck. Not exactly a final goal, but still a sense of accomplishment.

Now we knew that our search area extended from this point fifty miles east and seventy miles to the south. We sat right next to the rock and drank our tea in the cool of the evening.

Chapter 15

Our third day was also another learning experience. We were working very close to the equator, so a couple times a year, the sun would be directly overhead. Then it would wander for a few months, to one side or the other. Then we would begin to see what we called 'dust devils.' A mysterious force would cause the air to begin moving in a circular direction, quickly gathering force. It would suck up sand and dirt, and almost looked like a living thing as it marched across the landscape, flinging sand and pebbles everywhere.

Tom had studied this kind of thing, and he told us that the odd thing about it was that for half the year, the dust devils would move in a clockwise direction, and for the other half of the year, they would move in the opposite, counterclockwise direction, so somehow those things were caused by the rotation of the earth, and when the sun was directly overhead, for a few days, there would be none.

Now you could see and even hear those things coming so it was easy to get out of the way, but there was another type, a much bigger force that we did not understand at all. What we called 'devil winds. You might be out working, or even driving, and look up to see this dark cloud rising out of the desert and moving rapidly towards you.

If you were caught out in it, you would experience a sudden darkness, with a howling wind that would surround you with a suffocating mass of sand and dirt, so thick you could not see through it, and it would be filling your ears and eyes and mouth with dirt and sand with such force that you would fall to the ground, helpless and nearly unable to breathe.

That is when I learned the value of the wool blanket, which was a light one, maybe only a quarter of an inch thick. Well, maybe it wasn't wool, but it looked like one of those old army blankets. The thing was that it had a certain weave to it, such that I could put it over my head, and sit down with my back up against a sand dune, or the tire of the car, and breathe through it until the devil wind passed, which could be a few minutes, or as long as half an hour.

I soon learned to keep it very close to me. Even if I was in the car, the windows closed and got all of my canvas patches closed up, the wind was so strong that it would force dust to come through the smallest of cracks, and I would sit in the car with the blanket over my head.

I kept a bandana tied around my neck that I could quickly wet with water from the canteen clipped onto my belt and breath through it. That was my backup plan, but the blanket worked much better. Anyway, that day, we didn't find any of the site locations marked on our maps.

We were still learning our way around, and we soon learned to watch for any sign that a camel caravan had passed this way.

The tracks would be filled quickly by the blowing sand but a trail of old camel dung, what we used to call 'cow pies' when I was a kid, would show that this was a desert road, for the nomads knew every inch of the desert. They knew every place you could travel and every place to find water.

We found a couple of their wells over the next year. Just some flat rocks piled, but if you carefully removed the top one you could look down in the hole, and if you let down a rope, the end of it would come back wet. We left them just as we found them, but we marked the location on our map. If we ever got caught out and ran out of water, it could be a lifesaver.

Although we didn't see any of the Touregs, we sort

of became aware of their presence, and a couple times, I thought I saw a face peering over the top of a sand dune, only for an instant, and gone.

It was on the fourth day; we found the first site location. There was a huge depression, sort of like a ravine, about a hundred feet deep.

I pulled up nearby and walked over to the edge. I was looking straight down a rock wall of a depression maybe five blocks long. The other side, maybe a hundred yards away, was a sand slope, and in between the bottom sloped up to each end, as though the wind would come down into it and more or less scooped it out. I could just see the location marker, over near the far end.

We could get the truck over somewhere close, but we had to run out almost a whole roll of wire to reach the bottom, where we ran three lines of charges. It took us most of the day, but at least we would have something to turn in at the end of the week.

We talked it over and decided that the biggest problem was that the site markers were too hard to see from a distance. The geologist had some wooden stakes about four feet long that they pounded into the ground a couple feet, and a sign holder that slipped over the top, with a flat piece of plywood they slipped inside.

Using a small brush and some black paint they would mark it **Prospect # 3, or Essby #7,** Whatever, we agreed that the whole thing was too hard to see from any distance.

So, the next day, Friday, we knocked off about midmorning, and found our way back to Marrakech, in midafternoon. We needed to talk with one of the geologists, and we lucked out. His name was Riley Donavan, a fellow about my age, lean and tan and fit. He had been out there a couple months already, he and another fellow, and they had developed their route in and out of the area. They had two of the fourwheel drive Land Rovers, and they were each pulling a little flat trailer, with an ATV, a four wheeled thing with big sand tires on it.

They had a certain area where they parked the cars, making camp, and riding out every day on the ATVs. They had more mobility than we did, and much easier to get one of those things out of a sand trench if they happened into one.

Riley was an interesting guy to talk to, and he told me the reason why we were working in that particular area. It was back during the war, when the Germans tried to take over Africa. They not only sent in Rommel and his men and his tanks. They had also sent some geologists looking for places to develop oil fields to supply their machines of war.

Someone had found some of their old ecords that showed some promise of oil in that area. The war ended before they actually proved up on anything, but that was the basis on which the agreement had been made between Global and the African company, which had its headquarters in Cairo, Egypt, a long way away.

Mac explained our problem, the fact that we found the site markers hard to see from a distance, so, they went to work. There was a shop and supply room out behind the office building, with all sorts of tools and materials.

I watched while they took one of the fourfoot wooden stakes and cut it in half, throwing the top half away. Now they came up with a piece of tin, also four feet long but about eighteen inches wide. Using tinsnips they cut into the middle part from each side, laying the stake on the bottom half of the tin and folding it around the stake to a point, much like the way we folded a sheet of paper to make airplanes, when we were kids.

Now they had a sturdy bottom that could be driven into the ground and to the top half they mounted a piece of thick Styrofoam. Mac even cut it so that it sort of looked like an X, and spray painted a bright orange, it could be seen from a distance, with the site number painted on it, so it could be easily seen.

We agreed that it was a solution, and Mac pointed out that the old wooden stakes were a hazard to the nomads as their horse or camel might stumble over it, throwing the horse and rider.

"No use making enemies of the Touregs." That became our policy, and it would pay off much later, in ways we could not imagine.

Chapter 16

We were developing certain routines, as we adjusted to our life in the desert. For one thing, we no longer had to get up and leave so early in the morning, since we now had our route worked out. For the first 30 miles or so, it coincided with the route used by the geologists. Beyond a certain point however, we had our own route worked out, for a couple reasons.

First, we didn't want to be driving through their camp, stirring up dust, and second, because we had found a route that seemed to be used by the Touregs. We kept hoping that we would get a glimpse of them. The geologist, Riley, had some of the new style signs made up, and they had gone back, pulling up the stakes, and replacing them with the more visible ones, so we were having better luck at finding the sites, and as a result, we usually had at least three sets of charts and graphs to turn in at the end of a week.

Of course, we never saw the results, but I asked Riley one day if we were doing any good. "Well, it's hard to say. The charts are read by a couple of experts in the office, and they tell me that they are seeing some possibilities, but as of yet, there is nothing that would warrant calling in a rig to drill a test well."

"How about you, Riley, do you think there is really an oil field out there?"

He thought about that for a minute. "It's hard to explain, but my feeling is that a long time ago, part of that area was a swampy, steamy jungle, with all kinds of plants and animals that all melted together in the swamp, producing a kind of carbon bearing soup that seeped down into the earth where it was subjected to the heat and pressure necessary to produce the thick, gooey, evil smelling mess that we call crude oil."

I thought that was a pretty good explanation, so I asked him. "What is it going to take to find it?" "Mostly luck. Deep in the earth, there would have to be a rock formation, that the oil would seep into, and it would need to be tight all around to keep it in, maybe with a layer of rock on the top."

"Yeah, I found one like that once, in Louisiana"

He saw me smiling, as I remembered. "A penny for your thoughts"

"Well, see, there was this girl"

"Aha, a romance blossoms"

"No, it wasn't like that. We only met a couple times. She just came walking out of the trees. She was about this big" I put my hand up to the middle of my forehead. "She had honey blonde hair and a few freckles on her nose, and when she spoke, it was like music playing"

"My, my, this sounds serious. Are you going to marry her?" "Oh, no, I only met her a couple times, and she sent me a pen pal letter once, but that was quite a while ago. I'm sure she doesn't even remember me now. It was just a fleeting moment in time, quickly gone."

That week, I saw, one early morning, tracks leading up to one of the new style location signs. Not camel tracks, they were clearly the hoof prints of a horse, and made very shortly before we got there, as no sand had blown in the tracks yet. You could see clearly that the rider had gotten off his horse and walked over to the sign. He probably pushed it back and forth to test its flexibility. At least that was the thought that came to my mind.

Mac explained to me that there was one tribe of the Touregs not involved with camels. "They are the warrior tribe.

There is another type of nomads that live to the

south, and these warriors are here to protect their fellow tribesman from harm. If there is a camel caravan through enemy territory, you can bet there are some men on horseback very near to protect them. if not, the other tribe would attack them and 'steal their salt"

Somehow, I liked that idea; that our Touregs could be the good guys.

`We all found our own weekend routine. Tom and Ernie had found a card players club, where guys and gals from all walks of life could gather. They all paid a fee to the owner of the building for the use of the tables, and they had a snack bar for food and drinks. I only looked in once, but the cards were not really my thing.

Most Saturday mornings, I would take the bus that went to the downtown area. I found the public Library, and I hung out there a lot, researching the history of the desert and the Toureg tribe. I found out that here were over two million of that tribe, but almost all of them lived in the big desert area to the south and east of us called Mali, and from there eastward, across countless miles of open desert. They had many places, large villages, and tent cities wherever there was an oasis, a place with trees and water.

It confirmed what Mac had told me, that none lived in our area. They were only infrequent visitors. Still, I was fascinated by their history and their style and the clothes they wore. Somehow, they had learned to make an indigo dye, and the loose-fitting clothes they wore were often dyed that certain shade of blue.

On Sunday afternoons, I would take the bus downtown. There was a certain sidewalk café, with a few tables out front, under a shade awning, and they served that odd drink I had developed a liking for, with a dash of rum, and goat's milk foam on top. I could sit there for a long time, just watching people coming and going. The normal street traffic was a mixture of everything.

What really caught my attention was the way the Arab men always seemed to be so much cooler, They had different arrangements of loosely fitting garments, but the simplest one, was like a long sheet. Just cut a hole right in the middle for your head to fit through, drape the long ends down the front and back, and tie a braided cord around the middle to hold it all together. You only needed a white t-shirt and white boxer shorts underneath.

Mac found a dance club that we could reach by bus on a Saturday night. A big dance hall, with a live band. Pay a 20-dollar entrance fee and dance the night away. It opened at seven and by eight there would be over a hundred people on the floor.

There were tables around the sides, and there was a bar and a lunch counter, and it was cool. A great place to spend the evening. We knew that there were some guys and gals that came there with the purpose of making a connection, but that was not our aim.

We didn't even have a car; not about to take some girl home.

We soon found a group with similar interests. They were only there because they loved to dance. I had danced a time or two, in high school, but now I was dancing with some gals that seemed to enjoy teaching me the newer dances. One young lady, especially, was determined to teach me how to polka. That is an odd dance, where you sort of hop a couple steps one way and then hop a couple steps the other way, and then you both hop the same way, and start to go in a circle, so we would spin our way around the floor.

We got really good at it, and there were some people that would see us coming, and laugh and get out of our way, and others would hoot and holler and urge us on Great fun.

Now, I have to tell you, that gal was homelier than a mud fence, but she had a cheerful attitude and seemed to cheer everyone up, including me, because I was sometimes a bit lonely.

Mac sort of teamed up with a tall gal that was teaching him how to waltz, and it was neat to watch them as they spun gracefully around the floor.

We were along in our second month, when the messenger boy showed up with a letter for me as I was sitting at the supper table, just having washed off the desert dust after a hard week. I could not believe it. I could not think of a single person who would write to me for any reason. I considered all the possibilities; maybe a distant relative had died, and they wanted me to attend the funeral. All kinds of thoughts ran through my head.

There was a postmark, a bit smudged, but I could make out the name, '**Juliet**' and I didn't know anybody by that name. Finally, I got up the courage to open it. I read that letter over, several times, in disbelief. It was from that girl in the swamp, and she ended the letter with **Wish you were here,** and she signed it '*jill*, with a flourish.

I could not believe it. After all this time to get a letter like that; then somebody reminded me that the postal service from the states to here was not very good, coming across the water by boat, and unloaded in docks, sometimes the wrong one, and needing to be reshipped.

Anyway, the letter had obviously seen better days, as far as the condition of it, but it was still readable, and Jill wrote that she was staying with some gal called Molly, and they both worked in a roadside diner in some little town called Juliet. She was doing fine, thank you, and she liked it there very much.

Now, I admit that I had sort of put the girl out of my mind, but that letter stirred up memories, and I yearned to hear her voice once more. I could barely remember the times I had met her in the swamp, but I would never forget the sun shining on her hair, he freckles on her nose and the sweet sound of her voice. Not being able to do that, however, I gathered up some note paper, and a pen, and wrote her a return letter. I wasn't much of a letter writer.

I could not go into details, because at that time our work was still considered classified, but I told her that I was doing some surveys in an African desert; that we spent weekends in town, and I wished I could dance with her. I could not think of much else to say but I ended the letter with **Wish I was there.**

I took it over to the office and I got the lady there to help me get it into an envelope, and addressed, and I paid extra to get it delivered air mail. I could only hope that after all this time, it would find her with good memories of me.

Chapter 17

Jill was doing just fine. With Molly's guidance she had developed a lot of friendships in the early morning breakfast gang, the guys and gals that came in often, some of them every morning. There was one old guy, especially, who had taken a shine to her. They called him 'Pops' Donnelly, and he was a retired farmer. For some reason, she reminded him of a daughter that he had long ago lost track of. That sometimes happened in life, but now, it was like 'Pops' had found a replacement. He just liked to hear her voice, so he would come in late every morning, and take a table over in the corner, and give her the order for his breakfast. When she came back with his second cup of coffee, she would sit down at his table and chat with him a while. He was a nice old guy and she liked to hear some of his stories about the good old days.

It didn't hurt that, while most of the guys left a quarter on the counter for her, he would often leave her a bill or two.

Working together, and sharing living expenses, their cookie jars, where they kept their tips, were over-flowing, so one morning, when they had a rare day off, Molly said, "Let's go shopping"

They ventured downtown, and stopped at a used car lot. There was a little red car there, well used, but it ran, and the tires were good, so together they shelled out 500 dollars and became car owners.

Molly had to teach Jill how to drive, and they went out to 'Pops' farm a couple times. There was an empty field where they could just drive around in circles while they practiced. Soon Jill took the driver's license test and passed with flying colors.

Jill was happy, thinking that things would always stay just as they were, until one day when the postman came in and handed her a letter, an airmail letter She had not seen a letter like that for a long time.

It was not until that evening, that she showed the letter to Molly, who looked it over and asked, "Why haven't you opened it?"

"I never had a letter like that, since the day when I got the news that my parents had disappeared, and I was being sent to live with my grandpa."

Well, this doesn't look anything like that. the return address is in Africa."

Molly finally convinced Jill to open the letter, and she sat down on the couch, reading the letter three times before she handed it to Molly, who read it and said, "I told you so. This guy is in love with you. He says he is away working, but he wants to come dance with you when he gets back." Jill remembered him as the nicest guy she ever met

Chapter 18 ═══════════════════════════

It is the little things I came to appreciate about the desert. The solitude, the absolute stillness. Not a sound to be heard anywhere. No distant rattle and roar of traffic. A morning when there was not even a leaf to rustle. No flutter of bird's wings. Not even a sign of those little desert lizards that I enjoyed watching as they skittered across the sand. A chance for a man to be alone with his thoughts. A time when he could take stock of his feelings and consider his options.

At the moment, I was content. We had faced everything the desert had thrown at us, the heat, the occasional wind, the constant need for water. We were used to it, even, you might say, comfortable with it.

I felt like we were becoming one with it, but not quite to the point of being a desert dweller. No, there still were some big things, like the morning showers on the weekends.

Anyway, this particular morning, we were going to a new location. We had been out here, now, for seven months, and had been to maybe half of our permitted search area.

We were probably about ten miles east of the boulder that marked the corner, and maybe a little bit south. I guess the reason we had not worked here was because it required a rather circuitous route to get here. The land here seemed to be a bit different. A lot of sand dunes, not high, but long and curving, row after row, all neatly aligned as though the wind here knew to always blow in a certain direction, so as to not upset the scheme of things.

The truck was out there somewhere ahead of me, and I had stopped for a bit, maybe just to get a drink of water. Sometimes I would just get out to stretch my legs. I was looking down this sort of long little valley that lay between two of those long, curving, sand dunes. Somewhere along in there, I seemed to see a hint of water, maybe a reflection or just some moisture in the air. In this dry land, you begin to notice any sign of moisture, as it is a rare thing.

I was standing there, absorbed with my thoughts, when suddenly a shadow fell across the sand dune in front of me. I looked up to see one of those gigantic clouds of dirt and sand towering over me, and I knew the devil wind was almost there. I ran for the car, and by the time I got the door open, there was fine sand already starting to swirl around me. I got in as quickly as I could, got the side windows rolled up and all the canvas closed, zippered and velcroid into place.

It wasn't enough. The wind was howling now and with such force that the car was rocking from side to side, and little puffs of dust were coming in here and there. I got my blanket over my head and gathered the edges together with both hands and sat there, content with just trying to breath, which was harder than it might seem, because there was so much dust in the air, even inside the car.

Outside, it was utter chaos, with dirt and sand and small pebbles flying through the air. It sounded like the car was being sandblasted, and I began to wonder if there would be any paint left. I had no idea how the truck was faring, and I knew the radio didn't work in a storm like this. Nothing but static.

All I could do was sit there, under the blanket, trying to breathe evenly, while I listened to the wind howling. It seemed to be getting worse instead of better. I don't know how long I sat there. It seemed like a long time, but probably about ten minutes had passed when I became aware of a different sound.

Instead of the random sound of pebbles hitting the car. I heard a rhythmic, **tap.. tap.. tap.** I peeked out from under the blanket, to see a hand, through the lower right-hand corner of the windshield. It was a small hand, and it was holding a stone. I watched, in disbelief, as it continued. I leaned forward, to see better, and there was a face connected to the hand. The face of a little girl. A most remarkable face, like some desert fairy tale come to life. As quickly as I could, I got the door open and pulled her inside.

Luck was surely with me, as the wind, which was going back and forth the whole time, seemed to pause for a moment as it changed direction.

Still, a cloud of dust came into the car along with the girl. It took me a minute to assess her condition. It looked like her ears were plugged full of dirt, and her mouth, her lips were cracked, her nose appeared to be clogged with dirt and she was having trouble breathing.

But when she opened her eyes, ... I will never forget that sight. She had the most beautiful eyes I had ever seen. The white so white, in contrast to the greenish gold of the pupils.

t was like a green fire burning there. I threw the blanket over the two of us and unknotted the bandana from around my neck. I drenched it with water from the canteen I kept clipped on my belt. I began to wipe the dirt from around her nose and mouth, but I saw her looking at the canteen, so I had to give her a drink, just a bit at first, and then I tried to get some of the dirt out of her ears.

Then she indicated that she needed another drink of water. A bigger one this time.

I wondered how in the world she had managed to survive out there in that storm. It was still blowing fiercely, and the car would rock, and the dust was swirling. It was hell outside, and I could not understand how any living thing could survive.

This was absolutely the worst storm I had ever been in. It just went on and on. I kept wetting the bandana, and now she took it from me and began to wash her face and brush the dirt out of her hair.

I began to see, even in the very dim light, just how beautiful this girl was. she had a round face, with very fine features, a slightly olive complexion. No freckles like white girls tend to have.

She had an absolutely flawless complexion. Only her cracked lips to mar her otherwise perfect face.

Once she had herself cleaned up to her satisfaction, she handed the bandana back to me and pointed at the canteen. Another sip of water, which she seemed to savor, and she handed the canteen back to me with a smile.

I could not believe it. She had survived in a storm that would have been the death of many, and she could smile as if nothing had happened to her. Eventually, I would learn that was the nature of the desert people. Whatever happened, just shrug it off, suck it up, and go on.

We sat there under that blanket until the storm finally blew itself out. Most of the time her eyes were closed. Perhaps she was resting. In retrospect, I would later believe that it was just the way they were taught. Conserve your energy until you need it. Once the wind stopped, we got out of the car, brushing the dust off. I gave the blanket a good shake, and folded it up, placing it in the back seat, ready for the next time.

I saw the little girl, who appeared to be about ten or twelve years old, digging round in the sand that had piled up next to the front wheel. She came up with one of those goatskin water bags. I had seen some of those in use. They allowed just enough water to seep through that the evaporation tended to keep the water cool enough to drink, even on the hottest of days.

It was obvious that the water bag was empty, so I went to the trunk, and returned with one of my water containers. I took the bag from her and rinsed it out. When she saw me pour a little water on the ground, she looked shocked. I turned both my hands palms up, to show it was no problem. I had plenty of fresh water.

The water bag had a braided cord that she slipped over her shoulder. She was ready to travel, but I put a finger up to show that I was not ready. She waited. Now this may seem odd, but here we were two complete strangers, who in no way spoke the same language, and yet there seemed to be some sort of silent communication between us.

For some reason, I decided to fill a plastic water container I had picked up somewhere. It was probably a freebie because it had some sort of advertisement on the side. It held about a quart of water and had some sort of a little arrangement on the top that you could twist and then take a drink without having to take the top off.

I don't know why, but for some reason I thought I

could just hand it to the girl, and she would go home, but she shook her head.

When I hesitated, she took me by the hand and we walked the length of that little valley that way, like two old friends out for a stroll.

I can't begin to explain the feeling that I experienced that day. Suddenly it came over me just how nice it would be to have a little girl of my own, that I could walk with in the park on a spring day.

About halfway, we passed a pond of water, lower down and she pointed at the pond, and she pointed at the water bag, and I knew she had gone for water and the storm had hit so suddenly that she had lost direction, ending up, by a miracle, at my car.

Years later, I would still be wondering how that could have happened, the odds against it were astronomical.

We came to the end of the little narrow valley, and over a rise, I suddenly saw a tent. Not just any tent. It was a blue tent and very substantial, there were ropes that tied it down to stakes driven into the ground. It had to be a very good tent to still be standing after that storm.

A man came walking from behind the tent. I knew immediately that he was a Toureg, dressed in the unique blue robes that I had seen in pictures at the library when I had researched the Toureg tribe. He also had that distinctive blue headdress, with a braided cord that circled his head, and the flap on the back to keep the sun off the neck.

He stopped just a few feet from me as we appraised each other. He was obviously startled to see his daughter in the company of a white man, and I was looking to see if there was a knife sheathed in the folds of his garment. I knew that they never went out without weapons.

The spell was broken when the little girl ran to him. Taking him by the hand, a stream of conversation took place, none of which I could not understand, but she was pointing at the water bag, and she was pointing at me. She took him by the hand and pulled him over until we were standing right in front of each other, almost close enough to touch. At no time did the man's expression change. He seemed to be inspecting me, as though he was looking for some excuse to pull out his knife and cut off my ears.

Nothing was said, that was just the feeling I had.

I didn't know what to say or do, and in desperation, I handed him the plastic bottle of water. He stood there looking at it like it might bite, and I tried to show him, twist this here and tip it up like this and drink.

He probably thought I as some sort of stupid clown that had escaped from the circus. It didn't matter, because a woman came out of the tent, and the little girl went running over to her. There was a lot of hugging and kissing going on and more conversation that I could not understand. The man and I both just stood there watching.

Now, I have to tell you that this was the most beautiful woman I had ever seen in my life. Just like the girl, only more so in the adult version. The perfect, slightly olive complexion, the delicate features of a round face framed by brown curls

I was transfixed with awe and when she walked over and gave me a hug, and kissed me on the cheek, I almost fainted.

She backed up a step and, pointing at the girl, she said "**oo-for-is**"

The little girl pointed at herself and said "**me, oo-for-is**"

Okay, I got it; the fact that she was telling me her name, but the sudden realization that she said the English word, 'me' gave me something to think about. Eventually, I would learn that there was much more to the Toureg people than one might expect.

They were very intelligent people, and learning another language was just one of many things they could do.

The conversation sort of lagged at that point. So, I just made the motion of going back to my car. The girl and I gave each other a little wave of farewell and I turned and walked away, leaving the man standing there with that plastic water bottle in his hand. He never said anything, and his expression never changed.

One day, I would come to know that was the Toureg way of dealing with something they did not understand.

As I walked back, I stopped where I could look down into that pond of water. For some reason, the mist that was rising over the far side had an oily look to it. Maybe it was just my imagination, but when I caught up with the truck, I asked Tom. "You know, I hardly ever ask for a favor, but I wonder if we could run a couple lines?"

"Sure, I remember we did that a couple times before, and it turned out well"

So they followed me, with the truck back to that little valley. We spent half a day running out a couple lines and setting off the charges. A couple times I saw the man peering over the top of a dune, watching us. When we finished, I set out one of those location markers, Using the brush and a little can of black paint, I painted on the sign **Euphoris # 1**

That was the closest I could come to an English spelling of the girl's name.

When we finished, I walked over the rise at the end of the valley. The tent was gone, and I never saw that family again, but I will never forget that little girl and her mother, and those eyes, so beautiful and fascinating. I wished I had a camera that day, so I could show people because there was no way I could describe them.

Somehow this became a turning point in our

experience here, as we could mark that day as the beginning of our good days in the desert. Prior to that day, it was all heat and sand, and sweat, but now we were on the upswing, and it could ony get better.

We got back to Marrakech earlier than usual on Friday afternoon, and turned in our graphs and charts, with no idea that there was one set in there that would change our routines quite drastically. Life would never be quite the same.

Chapter 19 ═══════════════

Saturday morning, and I had barely set down to breakfast, when Riley came in, and took the chair opposite me at the table. We exchanged greetings and he watched me eat. He wasn't saying anything, but I could tell that something was bugging him, so I took a last bite out of my toast and pushed what was left of my breakfast aside.

"What's up, Doc?" I said, trying to relieve the tension with a little humor. It didn't work. "Out there, this week, you did something different" he said, "You deviated from the plan; something you never have done before."

It only took me a second to realize what he was

referring to. "Yeah, well, we had done that a couple of times before, in the states, but never here. It's just that once in a while, I get a notion and ask Tom for a favor, and he goes along with it. If we're in trouble, it's my fault, not his"

"No, it's not anybody's fault" He laid a copy of a report on the table, so I could see the name at the top. "I have to ask you, why here? And why this name?"

He was pointing at the header on the report. It said **Euphoris, number One.**

"Well, that was the little girl's name, she said **me, oo-for-is.** And that was the closest I could come to spelling it in English"

He had a serious look now. "Are you putting me on? How could you find a little girl in that desert? Nobody lives out there"

"Maybe not, but I couldn't tell her parents that. I don't speak the Toureg language"

"What, you talked to some Touregs? i been here for

a while and I never met anyone who ever talked to a Toureg. If you even get a glimpse of one, they vanish like the wind."

"Well, it wasn't much of a conversation. I only understood one word, and anyway, I didn't find her, she found me. I was hiding under my blanket, in the car, in the worst devil windstorm ever. She knocked on the windshield with a stone, and I let her in. Not much of a story, really."

He folded his arms on the table and gave me that look. He knew I was stringing him along, so I had to start over and tell him the whole story.

When I finished, I told him, "I wish you could have seen that girl, and her mother, oh, my, the most beautiful woman I ever saw"

"Okay, I understand that now, but why did you pick this spot?" He pointed at the report again, and I told him that when I looked at the murky water in that pond, there was sort of an oily mist rising at the far edge. "It really was just a hunch, nothing more" It was my turn to ask questions now. "Why, what is so special about that spot?"

"The two guys that read those graphs came and rousted me out of bed this morning. They say this is the first evidence that there might be oil located on our permit. Not enough to call in a test drill, but it could be the edge of something bigger" "I see. What do we need to do about it?" "I hate to ask you guys to give up your weekend, but time is of the essence.

The pressure from higher up is increasing. The big boss has already been called on this, and he told me to get my rear in gear."

As I was gassing up the car, I saw that riley had the rest of our crew out in the yard, and Riley was telling them to load more than usual of chart and graph paper. Take enough charges and detonators for an extra dozen runs" This already sounded like more than a weekend, maybe more than a week.

We led off, Mac and I, in the car. Riley had asked me if I could find the location and I told him maybe, but I was sure that Mac knew the way. Tom and Ernie followed in the truck, and Riley and his pal were in one of their Land Rovers bringing up the rear. Everyone was caught up with the idea that the time was important. We didn't know why, but it was like a race across the desert. We had about sixty miles to go, and we made it in a little over three hours.

We parked on the same spot where I waited out the storm and I walked with Riley up the little valley between the dunes. He climbed every dune in every direction, including the direction where the blue tent had been.

Then he came back, and got things organized. The other geologist, whose name was Willy, would help him lay out a search pattern. I would follow behind, with as many of the site location signs as I could carry, and Mac would help Tom and Ernie get the truck in position to lay out the first lines.

Riley and Willey had a hundred-foot tape measure, and one would stop while the other would pull out the tape as far as it would go, then he would make a mark in the sand with his heel and they would advance again, as soon as he had drawn it out on the clipboard he carried. Every so often, they would call, and I would pound in one of those site markers.

By the end of the day, I began to see the pattern. He was making a big circle, not around the pond, which was the starting point, but rather around some point beyond where the tent had been. The furthest point of the circle was probably about a thousand yards beyond the tent.

He wanted us to run two lines at each site location, and it took us seven days to do it all, working extra-long shifts. It was hot and dry and sweaty work, and we did not get back into town until noon Saturday.

I Showered and napped all afternoon; had supper and slept the night away.

Then I had all day Sunday to get rested up and it was a good thing because by the time we finished breakfast on Monday morning things were already happening. There were cars in front of the office. I saw Riley talking with a couple men our front and he gave me a thumbs up. A semi came up the lane, with a bulldozer on his flatbed. A big one. He made a circle around the yard and stopped, pointed to go out again. Then a big guy, who I thought might be the boss man, since he had on a hard hat with the word **BOSS** painted on it, pointed at Mac and said "You, get in that truck, and get him just as far as you can go.

Mac quickly climbed up in the cab, just as another semi pulled in the yard, making the circle and stopping close by.Tthe BOSS pointed at me. "You, get in this one and follow. Don't let him get lost."

Okay, but first I ran over to the car, and retrieved a jerry can full of water. Then I climbed up in the cab of the truck and the driver had the truck in motion even before I got seated.

At the time I didn't understand the reason for the big rush, but it was infectious. I could not believe I was in a semi-truck racing across the desert at break-neck speed. Of course, it slowed down as the going got tough, but we made it, I guess, about 35 miles before the lead semi crossed a flat area of soft sand, and the truck went down to its axles in the soft sand. The driver just shut the motor off, got out and climbed up in the cab of the big bulldozer and backed it off the trailer. Mac walked the ground for a way, finding some more solid ground about fifty yads to the left, and they started from there, as the bulldozer began carving out a road.

We parked right there, and I watched as my driver pulled down a couple ramps at the back of the truck, and backed the road grader carefully off the truck. I handed the jerry can of water up to him, and I climbed up to get in the cab.

The bulldozer would follow the route for a ways, but when one of those little sand dunes got in the way he would go to work with that big blade, pushing sand this way and that way, until there was a good wide opening.

We were following along behind, grading the sand, and starting to make something that looked like a road. We still had about fifteen miles to go, but by mid-afternoon, we were at the site. We stopped then, took a break, and all had a drink of water. I looked back down the new road then, to see something like a big steam roller, the was packing the road down, and there were trucks following that had loads of gravel.

This had to be a serious undertaking, as I thought of all the expense, with all the equipment involved.

Before long, a Land Rover arrived with the BOSS. There was a quick conference, and he pointed at me again, "You, catch the next empty truck going back. In the supply shed there is a fifty gallon barrel of lubricating oil for the equipment."

The first semi was still setting there, still stuck in the sand, as nobody had time to pull it out.

During the next couple days, I made several trips back and forth, like an errand boy. "Get this" and "we need that' Everything imaginable was going down that road. I saw a semi with a cook shack on the flatbed, and the cook with his arm out the window.

By the third day, there were fuel tankers and water tankers on that road, and they didn't really need me there anymore, but I watched for a while. It was then that I found time to talk to the boss, and he filled me in. Seems that when Global and the African oil company made their agreement, and got the permit from the Government, there was a codicil written in. They had to prove marketable oil by a certain date, or the permit would become null and void. That date was at the end of this month.

Friday, I watched as the drill rig came rolling up the road. The bulldozer was preparing the site for the first test well to be drilled.

I caught a ride back to town on an empty truck. At that time, I still did not have an inkling what an impact that would have. The thing was that the reports listed me as the one who discovered the site of the first oil discovery in that part of the country.

Now, on a weekend, I would try to get as far away from the oil business as possible, My interest was developing more along the lines of desert survival. I went to one of the Arab clothing stores and bought one of those white sheet outfits. The loose-fitting garment that went on over your head and then wrapped around you, with a braided cord that you tied loosely in front to hold it in place.

This one even had the shoulder things that hung down over your arms on each side, as far as your elbows. I also purchased one of the turbans. It is hard to describe, but imagine you took a pillowcase and rolled it up tight and coiled it around and around until it was flat, and stitched it together to keep that shape, and then added a flap around the back of your head to protect your ears and neck form the heat of the sun.

I probably don't describe it very well, but it was just a fun thing at first. I was trying it out on Sunday afternoon, as I sat in the shade in front of that sidewalk café, enjoying my favorite drink. Now, I had a pretty good tan, and I thought most people would have to look twice to tell that I was not a native. I also did not know how the desert grapevine worked, for some reporter from the local paper tracked me down. He not only knew who I was, but he had a camera, and he talked me into standing up in front of the café, in my Arab outfit, and with the café name right over my left shoulder. I thought that it was most likely just a small local scandal sheet of some kind.

Guess again, this was a big newspaper, with great circulation, and all of a sudden, I was famous. My picture, with the title, **Local man discovers first oil field in the empty quarter.**

Anyway, we still had a job to do, with about a third of our permit still not worked, so we were busy the next couple weeks, doing our thing.

This was an area that was quite different, as far as the topography was concerned. Less loose sand, more rocks, some sticking up out of the sand like sentinels, twenty or thirty feet tall.

Still, just a normal work area for us, but a couple times I caught a glimpse of a white horse and a blue turban, before they quickly disappeared behind a hill.

Nobody else seemed to have seen the horse and rider, so I kept my mouth shut.

One Friday, as we headed back to town, we drove around past the first oilfield and I was delighted to see one of those big walking bean pumps working away, up and down, as it pulled crude oil up from the depths beneath **Euphoris number 7.**

Chapter 20

Things were different now. Whether I like it or not, things have changed. Now, when I walked down the street, there were occasionally, people that knew me. The three China men having their conversation on the corner, would stop talking and point at me.

The children no longer offered their brochures. No one leaned out of their kiosks and gave me information. Even though I dressed in that native costume, they all seemed to know me as the foreigner who came to find oil on their land. I could not be sure if they admired it or hated me for it.

The good news was that my drinks at the café were now free, the proprietor having told me that the picture in the paper with the café name over my shoulder had increased his business by 20%.

Well, I guess I was good for something, after all, and I sometimes lingered over a second drink. So, it was, one fine afternoon, that I was not too surprised when a nicely dressed young man came out of the crowd and took the seat at the other side of my table. He didn't say anything; he just sat down and placed his hands on the table, one on top of the other.

As I knew from my studies, that was the Toureg way of showing that he had no weapons. it was to be a peaceful conversation.

Looking closer, I saw that he had the olive complexion and the fine features of a Toureg man. He said nothing, so I put my hands on the table, just the way he did, to show that I was willing to talk. Finally, he broke the silence. "You have met the girl."

I knew at once who he was referring to, and I said

"Yes, I have." Her mother is my cousin, and they only came this far to visit me."

I probably looked surprised, as I had no indication that any of that tribe ever came to town.

"I am what you might call a rebel, you see, I had no desire to live my life, with camels or horses, so I am here in University, my second year."

"I had no idea that the men of your tribe are allowed to do that."

"Oh, yes, we have a form of progressive government in place these days. They encourage all children to seek education."

"Even the children?"

"Yes, even so. Even **oo-for-is**. She says to tell you that she is learning much English and she sends you, her love."

I was touched. "Thank her for me and tell her that I am very fond of her, also." I was being very careful here, as I knew the wrong words could quickly end the conversation.

"There is a reason why I am here. You may sometimes see a horseman watching you."

"Yes, that has happened a couple of times."

"I am to inform you not to be threatened. They are there for your protection, not to harm you."

"I'm sorry. I do not understand."

"The land where you search for oil is a border area, sometimes disputed by the Berber tribe to the south. Without protection, they might try to stop you, or harm you in some way."

"I see, but why do I deserve such protection?"

"The girl's father is a cousin to the Chief of the tribe. He is a powerful man who rides a black Arab stallion; an equally powerful horse that can run fast as the wind. In the States, he would be worth a million as a racehorse."

"Now, I understand, but tell me this, how are you involved?"

"No, of course you would not understand, but you see, the Government of this country has certain laws that favor the Toureg tribe. One of them says that 5% of the profits from any oil found in this area, is to be paid into a fund that is set up to provide for the education of the children.

So, you see, you are paying for my education as well as that of **oo-for-is**"

He removed his hands from the table, indicating that our talk was over.

Before he left, he smiled and said "If you have any great need, just call the University office, and ask for **Ef-in-ould**. We, of course have lengthy last names, but you would not remember them. However, the office manager is a cousin, so they will know where I can be found"

He disappeared into the crowd, leaving me to

wonder just how many of that tribe had been educated and infiltrated into such positions. If they had members in the University, it would be reasonable to assume that they had members in the higher offices. Perhaps some of them were Senators or Congressmen. How else would they get a law passed, giving them a percentage of the oil profits?

Anyway, our conversation brought back memories of the day when that little girl and I walked hand in hand; one of my best memories ever, but that made me think of my other best memory, the day when I was talking with Jill, back in what seemed now like a lifetime ago.

I had never received an answer to the airmail letter I sent her, and I had to believe that was the end of it. I could only hope that she was doing all right.

****

But Jill was not doing all right.

In the late afternoon, a copper-colored cloud had gathered over the little town of Juliet.

Molly and Jill watched it from the front porch. There were dark expanses within, that were all roiled up, they seemed to be going in a circular motion, and there were flashes of lightning. It was like the gods above were gathering their forces, preparing to unleash their wrath on the puny humans below.

The air on the ground was deathly still, as though waiting for something to happen, as though it was hoping for the best, but expecting the worst.

Suddenly, the air was split by a terrible sound, the town siren; not with the steady wail that called the volunteers to a fire, but with a rising and falling wail, starting from a low note, and rapidly increasing in volume until it reached an ear-splitting peak. Then it would drop for a second, only to start over again, imparting a sense of urgency, a warning.

Molly and Jill left the porch and ran for the diner,

only a block away. They were met by a group of customers, and by their boss, who shouted, "Follow us.. Pete Briggs has a bomb shelter in his back yard" No time for questions, they ran as fast and hard as they had ever done. It was only a couple blocks, but Jill was already out of breath when they came through an open gate.

There were already people there, and they got in line, as each one was guided through a hatch and down a ladder into a room below, lit rather dimly by a couple of light bulbs housed in wire mesh, wooden benches lined the four walls, so, Molly and Jill took a seat and watched as more and more people came down the ladder.

Soon, all the benches were full, and still people came. It was standing room only, and there was some shuffling around as men gave up their spaces on the bench, to let the ladies sit down. She heard the man on the ladder say, "that's it" and the metal lid slammed shut.

For a while, it was quiet, as each person was lost in their own thoughts, wondering what might be happening to their homes and businesses outside. Finally, a man broke the silence. "We all thought Pete was nuts, back during the cold war, when he decided to build a bomb shelter, but I'm glad he did" There was a unanimous shaking of heads and murmurs of "That's right" Another man spoke up. "I wish he was still here, so we could thank him in person" Somebody led a prayer of thanks, followed by a chorus of 'Amens'. After what seemed to be a long enough time had elapsed, the man on the ladder, turned the wheel, releasing the lock and he opened the hatch just enough to peek out. He quickly closed it again and somebody asked him, "what did you see?"

"Nothing but the wind and tree branches blowing

past. They were sailing straight across, as though carried by an invisible hand."

A feeling of dread finality invaded that little space in the ground. It was like everyone knew that this was the big one. The hundred-year storm that everyone had known would come someday but I were hoping it never would.

It seemed like ages, but finally, the man on the ladder opened the hatch. It's over."

One by one they emerged from the shelter, to survey the scene of desolation around them. their happy little town now lay in shambles, the tornado having made its way right through the center. There was not a single building in town that had escaped at least some damage. There were some that were repairable, but many were not.

There were boards and debris piled everywhere, and they had to find a way through it to get back to the highway. The diner was totally smashed; just a pile of broken boards, with an occasional glimpse of a table or a stool, where the customers used to sit and talk while Jill and Molly poured coffee.

"That's it" said Ray, "I'm done cooking. My brother has a little ranch down in Texas. He has invited me a couple times to join him, so I'm going to trade in my apron for a hat and spurs."

Molly's house was not quite that bad, but there was a big tree that had been uprooted, causing it to fall through the roof, so now there were branches inside the kitchen and living room. The two bedrooms were a shambles, the windows blown out, and the plaster in piles on the floor. They salvaged what they could, some clothes and sheets and a quilt or two.

Jill found the drawer where she kept her things. The bank pouch was still there, in which she kept her most important papers, her bank statements and check book, and her pay stubs and birth certificate. But she did not find the card Chris had given her, or the airmail envelope with the return address. Their little car seemed to be okay, a few dents here and there, so they just threw what belongings they could salvage into the back seat and started driving. They had no idea where they were going, but it seemed to be, mostly north and west, away from the swamp, and away from their happy life in a happy little town. They stopped only for gas, and an occasional rest stop, driving through several little towns, but none of them looked like home to them.

A couple days later, as they entered another small town, it was decided for them. Their little car gave up. It just shuddered and died. They walked into town, and there was a restaurant, with a help wanted sign. What else could they do?

Chapter 21

I learned something this morning about human frailties. All this time we had been working together, I had never spent time with Ernie and Tom on the weekends. I did my thing and Mac did his, meeting occasionally at the dancehall on Saturday night.

I had never given any consideration to our coworkers and what they did to occupy their time. But, this morning, Tom sat down at my breakfast table after everyone else had left. He needed someone to talk to, and I listened, as he told me that Ernie had a problem. He had always made a joke out of 'looking for Sadie' but it seemed that somehow, that was a serious thing to him.

He became lonely and despondent, and when he got depressed, he turned to alcohol. He would disappear on a weekend, and Tom, as his only friend, would go looking for him, sometimes finding him late at night, passed out in some bar.

Well, now I knew why Ernie was often glassy eyed on Monday mornings, and seldom said anything during the week. He had a problem and Tom told me that the only thing he could think of doing was to pack it in. "Our contract with Global is almost over.

Another week or so, and I am going to take Ernie back to the states. If I don't, he will die here, from drinking himself to death, if his liver does not fail him first."

I agreed with him that it was a good idea, but it got me to thinking, and I dug around to find my passport and visa. Maybe it might be a good idea to get them up to date, just in case.

It was a Monday morning, and we still had a

portion of our permit to work. As we drove out the now well- traveled road, I thought about the first day; that very first time we drove out into the desert; the apprehension, and the pang of fear I felt deep inside, when the pavement disappeared, and we passed that sign that said, No services for the next 250 miles. Little did I know that there was a one missing from the sign. It should have said 1250.

Now there was a macadam surface to drive on as far as the oil field. As we passed it, I saw that there were now three of those big pumps working and they were preparing the site for another one.

From there on, we were on our own, but it was a good solid surface. No problems and we were at our search location by noon. This was a large flat area, sort of a tableland that was higher than the surrounding area. You could stand on a hill and see out across the desert to the south for a long way, until it just faded into the distance, the greatest expanse of nothing I had ever seen.

We had been warned however, that that was the land of the Berber tribe, and we had been warned not to go within ten miles of their border, which was well marked on our map. I could not imagine why any of those countries would be worth fighting over. There was nothing out there, and I knew that the nearest town in that direction was Timbuktu, which was a thousand miles from here.

This was the furthest part of our permit area, and the geologists had been here, mostly as a routine, just finishing up the details, as they saw no reason to believe that there was any oil here.

We did our jobs like always, laying out some lines, shooting off some charges, and making some graphs and charts like we always did, but without any real enthusiasm.

Mac and I had our evening tea, like we usually

did, and I saw Ernie sitting with his back against the truck with his head in his hands, and Tom trying to cheer him up.

Later, a couple of things happened. As I went for a walk in the cool of the evening, I was looking out over that desert again, to the south, marveling at the total emptiness of it, when I caught a glimpse of movement over to my left, where a pile of broken rocks protruded. There was one of those stone sentinels just beyond that, and in the space between, I saw a horse and rider, my first reaction was fear, because of the warnings about the Berbers, but then, reality, for it was a black horse, and the rider was dressed in the beautiful outfit of a Toureg.

I had glimpsed men on white horses before, a couple times, but I quickly realized, this was the Chief, the cousin of the girl's father, the one who rode the great stallion. Of course, I ran over there and looked, but he had vanished like the wind.

That night I had a dream. I saw the weird little man, in the rusty red shirt, I was trying to run away from him, but as I remembered in the morning, he seemed to be beckoning to me, and I had the feeling as I thought about it later, that he was telling me to come home.

Now, always before, when I saw the little man, with the little wooden crown nestled in his frizzy hair, I he had pointed out to me, oil here, or no oil there, but this time it was Mac that made the discovery.

We had done a morning set and had moved to a more westerly location, still on that high tableland, but now you could look to the west, across a broad valley several miles wide, and see in the distance, a mesa of red rock that seemed to run for miles, not high, but surely a red sandstone bluff, like I had seen one time in the Utah desert.

Mac walked right out to the edge. He was standing on the very top edge of a dark rock face, he was looking down into one of those depressions like we had seen before, where the wind seemed to have scooped out the sand, blowing this way and that, but leaving an empty place with ends that sloped up so that you could walk down into it from ither end. Mac came walking back to the car, telling me that he thought he saw an oil seep at the bottom of the depression. Just like that I knew, and I told him, "you get the sign, and I will get the paint and the brush."

It only took ten minutes to walk down into the depression. The smell of crude was so powerful there that we could barely stay long enough for Mac to paint a name on the sign.

We didn't even take time to make a chart or anything. We just left the truck there and raced back to town, all four of us. We found Riley in the office. We were all talking at once.

Finally, he said. "Wait, one at a time" so I said, "Oil seep" and I stuck my fingers under his nose. They were black from when I stuck my hand in it, not believing it myself. He took a big sniff, and said, "Good Lord" and things began to happen. He was on the phone, and by the time we managed to get a restroom stop, and could grab a sandwich, Willy was there. They didn't even bother with my car,. "Too slow" so we were on our way again, me and Ernie with Willy and Tom and Mac with Riley.

It was another race across the desert, but it gave me a chance to talk to Ernie, and he confirmed what Tom had told me. He had relatives, and friends, back home that he needed to visit. He needed to go home, and they had already taken their passports in to be updated.

Somehow, just talking about going home seemed to cheer him up, but it had the opposite effect in me, as I had no home to go to, and nothing to look forward to, back in the states.

We made record time back to the site, and we spent

a couple more days laying out lines around the oil seep, but it was just routine. It showed us where the reservoir of oil was, and there was no doubt about it.

The four of us got in the truck on Thursday and drove back to town.

On Friday, Tom and Ernie turned in their resignations at the office. They told us they had booked tickets on a cruise liner, one of those big boats, with hundreds of people, entertainment, and lots of food, I bid them goodbye, hoping that Ernie might find his Sadie on the boat.

That left just me and Mac, and on Sunday afternoon, we went downtown. We both were wearing our loose-fitting white robes. Now I was about five foot ten and Mac was at least five inches taller than me. Not exactly Mutt and Jeff, but people were staring at us. We knew why, as we were enjoying our drinks, the reporter showed up. He talked us into standing up in front of the café, to get our picture taken, which made the owner so happy, I thought he was going to have a conniption fit, or something.

We should have been happy, but we weren't. The fact was that we were on the top, and there was nowhere to go but down. Almost two years we had been there and what did we have to show for it?

We knew we had a bank account somewhere, and with all our pay, and the bonuses for bringing in two oil fields, it might be a lot of money, but you can't buy happiness, and I wasn't happy.

I told Mac that I thought I needed a change of scenery and asked him if there might be someplace that he might like to go. He thought about that for a while, and then he told me, "For several years, I worked on a cargo ship as a deck hand. I visited almost every port around the Mediterranean Sea. from Gibraltar to Cairo.I jumped ship there and joined a company that hauled freight across the desert, from there to here. Made a dozen trips, before I got tired of driving and signed up with Global as a guide.

So, I guess what I am saying is that I have seen about as much as I care to, of this part of the world." He asked me if there might be someplace, I would like to go. "I don't know. I think, like you, I have had enough of this part of the world, but I don't really know any place to go, except maybe back to the States."

'Well," he said, "I always kind of thought I might like to see the Rocky Mountains." That was all it took. The next day, we handed in our resignations, and booked passage on a ship bound for the States. Not one of those big cruise ships, but definitely one much, much better than the one I arrived on, when I came to Africa.

Chapter 22

We had been given three choices when we went to purchase the tickets for the cruise to the States. We could land in New York, Miami, or New Orleans. I chose the latter, since our only goal at the moment was the Rocky Mountains, and it seemed to involve the least driving time from there.

It had been a quiet and peaceful cruise. Lots of time to work on my journal, while I made an effort to put on paper all the things that had happened in Africa. Someday, I had the crazy idea, I might even put it all in a book, and have it printed, but then, I would quickly remind myself, that I had no family, no one who would be interested in reading it. Oh, well, I have to do something to pass th time.

Mac spent much of his time in a deck chair, reading a book. I had not realized how well learned he was; he had never mentioned going to school, yet he could strike up a conversation with almost anyone, about whatever subject seemed to interest them.

As a result, he made a lot of friends during the voyage, while I made very few. I was more of a listener. There was one rather sweet young lady that sat at the captain's table every evening. We were invited twice to dine at that table, and that young lady seemed to enjoy talking to me, while most everyone else at the table was either talking to Mac or listening to the conversation between him and the captain.

It was with some trepidation that I faced my future as we made port in New Orleans. I had no goals, no purpose, no direction in life. It was lucky for me, that

I was traveling with Mac, who always seemed to have a purpose.

Every time I thought I would just sit down and watch the world go by, he would come up with a goal for the day, and I had to get in step to keep up with him.

So it was, that as soon as we had cleared customs and immigration, he suggested that we should find a hotel, get a couple nice rooms, and enjoy the atmosphere of New Orleans while we got our land legs working. There was a big celebration going on, with a daily parade, lots of noise and streets crowded with people.

After the quiet and isolation of the desert, I was not ready for all that commotion, and soon I was telling Mac that we should hit the road.

He considered this a moment and responded by changing direction. Once away from the main street, and more into a regular business district, it did not take long to find a car dealership. This one sold several different models, including Buicks and Jeeps

There was a whole row of cars right along the sidewalk. Mac asked me if I had a preference. "Well, I don't know, if we get into the mountains someday, I might prefer a four- wheel drive. I used to drive a Jeep Wrangler, but it was a company car."

It didn't take long to find a Jeep Wrangler in the lineup. Mac opened the door and looked inside. He quickly backed out. "Nope, too small, and it only has two doors. What if we should find somebody to ride with us?" I currently had no illusions about anybody riding in a car with us, but knowing Mac, it could happen, so I agreed. "Okay, which one do you like?"

We strolled a little further down the line, and he stopped by a red model. It looked like a fire engine, and the sign in the window said Grand Cherokee with a price that would choke a horse. "Too much, both color and price."

"You know we have plenty of money, and we can go half and half."

"Maybe so, but I might want to buy something else someday, and besides I don't like to attract attention when I drive down the street. You could see that thing coming a mile away."

Okay, we kept walking up and down the rows of cars, stopping here and there to look inside or to kick the tires. We were about midway down the third line of cars, when I spotted one that caught my eye. It was a light sand color and the sign in the window was less than half of the red one.

Mac walked around it, opened all four doors and looked inside. I kicked the tires, and they didn't kick back, in fact they looked to be nearly new.

As if by magic, a salesmen appeared, with the usual spiel, probably claiming that it was only driven by his granma to church on Sunday.

I wasn't paying much attention to what he said.

Mostly I just liked the color, as it reminded me of the color of the sand in the area where I first saw that blue tent.

Anyway, we signed some papers, and each wrote out a check, and in a couple hours we drove out of there, proud owners of a Jeep Cherokee, not the Grand model, but I liked this one better. The Grand model had leather seats, but this one was a sort of a tough fabric, which was cooler to sit on a hot day. Also, the color accents were brown and dark blue. Not that it mattered, but Mac liked it in a functional way, while I liked the color, so we were both happy.

Now, our problem was that we had no idea where we were going, our only inclination was to end up in the Rocky Mountains. We went through a drive-in, something we had not seen in years, leaving with a sack of junk food, probably bad for us, but delicious. We found a shady place to park while we ate and talked about our options. I had an atlas road map that the salesman had given me.

My bonus I guess, for he was a happy guy, might have made his day with that sale. I was hoping that it didn't mean he had sold a lemon. While we ate, I studied the maps and decided that there were three possible routes that we could take to get to the Rockies. I traced each one with my finger; quite a long drive, whichever way we went, but suddenly my finger stopped on the name of a certain town. A name I remembered from the return address of a pen pal letter I had received long ago. Mac noticed my hesitation. "What's up? You look like the cat that ate the canary." "No, I'm just surprised. There is a name here that I didn't expect to see, that's all."

Now, his curiosity was aroused, and I had to tell him the whole story, about the girl in the swamp, and the way she had signed her letters, ***wish you were here.***

Now he was really interested. "I didn't know you had a secret love. All the times we danced with girls, you never seemed to take any of them seriously." "I know. I can't explain it. There was something about her, something different. It was like she seemed to know me, without even being introduced."

"Maybe we should go look her up. Is she still in the swamp?"

"No, she wrote in her last letter, that she was working in a diner, with a girl named Molly"

"Okay, we have a name and a town, and it's on the way. We might as well look her up"

"It's probably just a waste of time. She probably does not even remember me."

"Doesn't matter. You were complaining about not knowing what to do. This gives us a goal, and you say it's on the road anyway.'

Like I said, daily goals were important to Mac, so I gave in, and we started out. Once we found our way out of town, it became sort of a joy ride. We had no work to do, no schedule to keep. We could take turns driving. Stop anytime for coffee or gas. If we were tired, we just found a motel and got a couple rooms. If it had a swimming pool, much the better. All that water, and you could just jump in it, after all those long months in the desert, where even the sight of a muddy pond was a rare thing.

As we worked our way up the highway, I kept my eye on that name on the map, Juliet, and as we got closer, I felt a tingle of excitement although I had little hope that the girl would remember me, or even want to talk to me.

So, it was mid-afternoon when we finally came to the sign that said **Juliet.** It appeared that there had been more to the sign, but it was badly broken, and the piece with the name was propped up by a broken piece of two by four.

We stopped in front of the only building on the

highway, and there was still a little sign visible, next to what once was a door. The sign said 'Diner, but there was nothing left of it; it was just like a pile of broken boards. Looking through the cracks, I could see a table and part of a counter with a stool or two.

We walked around the building, looking for a back entrance, but that was worse. It was obvious that there had been a disaster, but where were the people?

About a block away, I spied a little house, and I had the thought that it might be Molly's house, as Jill had mentioned sharing a home. But the building had a big tree crashed down in the middle of the roof. I could not imagine the force that had done a thing like this. We got into the Jeep and drove on, finding a street that went into town. On both sides of the street were houses in various stages of demolition, damaged beyond repair, and in the process of being torn down.

I told Mac, "Well, that's it. End of story. At least we

tried." But Mac was not so easily deterred. "You give up too easy, buddy. Give it a little longer.

We can hang around here a day. We're in no hurry"

"Okay, but we will have to sleep in the car. There is no hotel in this wreck of a town."

What was I complaining about? I used to like sleeping in the car. The easy life was getting to me already.

But what was another day? We could be on our way in the morning. I would just swallow my disappointment and we would be on our way to the Rocky Mountains.

Guess again.

Chapter 23

We found our way to a park. Here, it was quite evident, - the path of the tornado, as one half of the
park was a mass of broken trees, stripped of their
branches and leaves, while the other half of the park
was relatively unscathed. There were a couple of picnic
benches, and one of those public restrooms, made of
cinder blocks, and I had, of all things, running water.
As we washed up, we joked about how we should have
had one of these that we could have set alongside the
road into the desert.

"We could charge a dollar to get in and we would
have made a fortune" Might as welllaugh about it,
but we knew the local people did not have anything

to laugh ab out. We only saw a very few walking about in the evening. "At least there is a chance that there may be someplace further along, where we can get some breakfast in the morning." Mac was always looking ahead,

We slept well enough in the car. I had a way of curling up in the back seat, with my feet over in the corner, and my travel bag for a pillow.

My duffel bag disappeared long ago. Mac slept in the front seat, although he was too long for it, and had to have one door open with his feet hanging out. I heard him a couple of times during the night, slapping at mosquitos that wanted to share his space.

We washed up in the restroom in the morning and drove on down the street, just as he thought, there was a part of downtown that was still standing, and one of the buildings was a café, with a few cars parked in front. We took a couple seats at the counter, and a waitress poured us a cup of coffee, without a comment. Of course, Mac soon had her talking.

Her name was Flo, so after a breakfast of ham and eggs, when she refilled our coffee cups, he asked her if she knew some waitresses by the name of Jill and Molly.

"Nope, sorry, I can't help you there. Half the people left here after the storm, and I just came in because my cousin has this café, and he needed some help."

No luck there, but I noticed an old guy at the far end of the counter, who seemed to be watching us. When Flo laughed as she poured Mac a third cup of coffee, he came over and took the stool next to me.

A nice old guy, he said "Heard you mention a couple gals who used to work at the Diner." "Yeah, I met Jill a couple times, before we shipped out. Just thought we might try to look her up."

"So, you're not trying to serve papers on her, or anything."

"Oh, no, nothing like that. she sent me a couple of pen pal letters, just being nice."

"Yes, Jill would do something like that. She was just a sweet gal. By the way, they call me Pops' Donnelly. I guess you could say I'm an old-timer around here."

I introduced myself and told him that Mac and I were just passing through.

"Well, those girls just got in their car and left town right after the storm. Headed west, I think. I kind of miss her, she used to sit and talk to me after breakfast. None of these gals here ever do that."

"I only talked to her a couple of times, but for some reason, I still remember her voice. She had the softest, sweetest voice. I wish I could hear it again."

I was ready to get in the car and head out, resigned to the fact that I would never see her again, but Pops looked me in the eye for a minute and said, "I think you're all right, so I guess I can tell you that she wrote me a note one time, telling me that they were alright, and had landed in a town somewhere west of here."

"Really? Do you know the name of the town?

He squinted like he was trying to remember. "Nope, don't recall."

My hopes were dashed again, but then he said, "I only live a couple miles out of town, but it you have time to stop by, I might have that address somewhere."

We followed him out of town. He had a nice little ranch house, and a barn, and I could see a few cows wandering around in the pasture.

"I'm retired now, rented the farm out, but I deep a few livestock around just for company." He didn't invite us in. We just sat in the car or a while watching some chickens in the yard, and some flies buzzing around a feed pail. It took quite a while, but eventually he came out and handed me a slip of paper. It was folded over, obviously having been in a drawer for a while.

It was hard to read, but I made out the name of a town. "Evers Ville?"

"Yeah, that sounds right. It's been a while now, and she only sent a brief note, wanted me to know that they were all right."

I got out the Road Atlas and searched up and down. Didn't see it, so I went to the index, found the name and it gave me the location on the map -C-6.

When I finally found it, I told Mac. "This is even a smaller place than Juliet, and it's on a back road, off the highway. I can't imagine how they could have gotten there." It only took Mac a moment to reason it out.

"It's still in the general direction of the Rocky Mountains, isn't it."

"Yes, I guess it's roughly about halfway there, but a long way from here."

"It doesn't matter, it gives us something to shoot for, like a target."

Okay, we thanked Pops and headed out. We still

had an afternoon of good driving on a highway, and that evening we found a nice motel with a swimming pool. I was becoming addicted now to water. Nothing like it, the wetness, the coolness. I was even learning to swim a bit, but still not ready for the deep end. We had a leisurely breakfast the next morning and got an early start, but now we had to take some back roads and we were having to work to find the way to that place.

"That 'Ville" in the name must mean it's a village, but how in the world did those gals find their way there?"

"Maybe they were just as lost as we are." It was past noon when we finally found the sign that announced **Evers Ville, population 149**.

Not much of a town, but just a few stores in the business district, and only one restaurant, so we parked and went in. it was dimly lit, and we didn't see any waitresses, just a lunch counter and a couple of booths, with only two guys in cowboy hats, seated in one of them. We took a seat at the counter, and in a few minutes a lady came out of the back room. She was as tall as me, with dark hair, and I wondered if this might be Molly.

"Howdy, fellas, you're a little late for the lunch rush. The special is all gone, but we might rustle up a sandwich or something, or maybe some pie."

When she said that, one of the cowboys in the booth waved to her and murmured something.

"Keep your shirt on, Junior. She's in the kitchen, cutting the pie. Be with you in a moment." She turned her attention back to us, well, mostly to Mac. He was giving her that smile, and he started to have a conversation with her. I don't know what they were saying, because just then this girl came out of the back room, she had three saucers balanced on one arm, with a slice o pie on each one.

She set one down on the counter and took the other two over to the cowboys in the booth.

Coming back, she looked at me, "Would you like a piece of pie?"

"Yes, Miss, I surely would."

She reached down, and placed a fork in front of me, along with the slice of pie. I must confess that pie was not what was on my mind right now, as I considered those honey blonde curls and the little freckles on her nose.

"You probably don't remember me, but we have met before."

She smiled at me, and it was like the clouds parted and the sun came shining through.

She sat down on the stool next to me. "Sure, I remember you. You're the nice guy who sent me an airmail letter once. I still have it, but I lost the envelope in the storm, so I couldn't write back"

My mind was in a tizzy. I didn't know what to say

or do, so I tried a bite of pie. "This is delicious. Did you make it?" Molly answered her. "Jill does most of the baking for us." She looked around, making sure the boss was not in hearing distance. "Most of the food here doesn't amount to much, but the bread and the pie is good.'

Jill didn't say much, she just sat there, with a little smile on her face, while I ate pie, and Mac and Molly carried on a conversation. I don't remember much of what was said, but when a couple cars pulled up out front, I heard Molly say, "We close at three, but we don't get off until we get the place cleaned up, so we will meet you at the park at four."

Chapter 24

We found the park, and there were some picnic tables there in a shady place under some trees and with a little creek that meandered by. We were both seated on one side of the table, when the girls showed up, carrying a couple of picnic baskets. Soon they had spread a tablecloth over the table and set out four paper plates.

"We do this almost every day." Said Molly, "When they close, the cook just throws out any bread that is left over, and whatever is left in the cool table, so we grab up some bread, and butter, and maybe lunch-meat and cheese, whatever we can find."

It might be leftovers, but it was delicious, and we

had not had anything to eat since breakfast, except that piece of pie. It was not the food that I would remember, though, in years to come. It was Jill setting there, across from me, just like we were old friends, and sharing bread together.

This was the sort of thing I had dreamed about all those long months in the heat and dust of the desert. The cool, shady place, the companionship that I longed for. I could hardly believe we were here, and already I was dreading the fact that this would not last.

We would have to leave and be on our way. She spoke up, in that soft voice, "You said in your letter, that you were in some desert, but I really didn't know where."

"Yes, we were in Morocco, in Africa." "Oh, I know where that's at. I did well in Geography, when I was in school, back before I was sent to live with Grandpa."

This was the first time she had spoken about her

past, so I tried to keep the conversation going. "What happened to your folks?"

"I don't know. They just left one day and didn't come back. Nobody would tell me anything. All they said was that I could not stay there by myself, and they shipped me off." I chewed on that a while. "So, when Grandpa passed; you were all alone."

"Yes, I still am, really, the only people I know are you and Pops and Molly."

"I guess we are in the same boat, sort of. My family is all gone and the only people I know are you and Mac"

At the mention of his name, Mac turned to us. "I was just telling Molly how much we would like to take these ladies to a dance."

"That sounds like a good idea."

"But we can't. there is no place to dance here. There is nothing here, nothing to do, the guys that come in to eat only talk about corn and cows and the weather, and if it is too wet to plow. If we try to talk to them, they look at us like we have two heads.'

As I was soon to learn, Molly was quite vocal about things.

I looked to Jill to see what she thought about it, and she was nodding her head up and down in agreement. "After Juliet, this place was such a disappointment. That storm just ruined our lives." "Why did you settle here, then?"

"I guess we took a wrong turn." Molly said, "maybe a couple wrong turns, and then our little red car just quit on us, leaving us stranded here on the edge of this place. It's like the arm pit of the world."

"What was wrong with your car? Couldn't it be fixed?"

"We never saw it again. it quit in the middle of the road, and they towed it off to some junkyard, somewhere"

Now, Jill didn't say much, and I could see that she

did not like to complain, but Molly was quite vocal. "No dances, no parties, not even a card game. I think these people here have some sort of religion that prohibits fun as a vice of some kind"

"We have been saving our tips" Jill said, "And we have almost enough for a bus ticket out of here." "But I gave you a check. Why didn't you use that?"

She smiled at that. "Yes, you are the only guy that ever gave me anything worthwhile, but you see, that was just a loan. I have that in a bank account somewhere, but I was just waiting to see you so I could give it back."

I was finding this all a bit depressing, but Mac and Molly went off to sit on the other park bench, so I changed the subject. "Well, if this is the worst thing that ever happened to you, what are some of the good things?"

"Oh, yes, there were some good days, before Grandpa started to lose his memory, and before the nice neighbors moved away. And then there was the day I met you, and the day we went to work in Juliet and the day I met Pops."

Now it was something special to be included in her list, but I said, "Yes, I met Pops. He's a nice old guy." "He was just lonely, you know.

He said that I reminded him of a daughter he had once, who had gone off somewhere, lost in the world and never seen again."

She looked like she was about to cry. I could not imagine a person who had this much compassion for someone. She swallowed it, though. "Now it's your turn. Tell me about your best day."

It didn't take me long to answer that. "Actually, I have two best days; the day I met you and the day I met the little girl in the desert."

That made her smile. "Tell me about the little girl. How did you meet her?"

"It's kind of hard to explain, but I was sitting in

my car, with a blanket over my head, in the worst sandstorm I ever experienced. It was the devil winds at its worst. Then I heard a tapping on the windshield. There was a little hand with a stone in it, and when I looked closer, I saw a girl's face attached to the hand."

Jill was getting excited now. "Who was she, and what did you do?"

"The only thing I could do was get her inside the car. The wind was howling, and dust was swirling everywhere. She got under the blanket with me, and I wet a bandana with water from my canteen and started to wash the dirt out of her nose and mouth and ears.

She could barely breathe at that point, but once she had a couple drinks of water out of the canteen, she opened her eyes and looked at me, and it took my breath away.

She had the most beautiful green-gold eyes you

could imagine, and when she took the bandana and washed her face, and brushed the dirt out of her hair, I could see that she was beautiful. A round face, and a flawless complexion, with brownish curly hair." Jill was clapping her hands. "This is the best story I ever heard. What happened next?" "Once the storm was over, she made me realize that she had gone out to fill her water bag, and when the storm came up so suddenly, she lost her way, and it was a miracle that she found the car. Otherwise, she would have perished, for sure."

Jill was leaning forward, wanting to hear more. "Yes, go on.What then?"

"Not much. I thought that, after I filled her water bag with fresh water, she would just go home, but she refused. She took my hand, and we walked up this little valley, just like we were old friends, and at the end of the valley, over a rise, there was a blue tent, and her father came walking out. He was dressed in the blue outfit of a Toureg, with the blue turban and all, and the way he looked at me, standing there with his daughter, I was afraid he might pull out a knife and cut my ears off."

"But he didn't, did he? You still have your ears." That got a smile from me.

"Well, maybe because the girl's mother came out of the tent, and they got together, with a lot of hugging and kissing. I could not understand a word they were saying, but the girl was pointing at me and pointing at the water bag. Then the mother, who was the most beautiful woman I have ever seen, came over and hugged me and kissed me on the cheek, and I almost fainted.

"Did they talk to you at all?"

"The lady pointed at the girl and said "oo'for- us, and the little girl ;pointed to herself and said 'me, oo-for-us."

"That was the only word that I could understand

was that one word 'me' but I found out later that the Touregs were very bright, and later I was told that she was in school." "So, what did you do?"

"Nothing, her father was still looking at me, like he was trying to decide whether to cut off my ears, my nose, or my hands. So, I said Bye, and got out of there."

"Well, that is absolutely the best story I ever heard, but there must be more to the story. Someday, you will have to tell me some more." Of course, I was elated, that she might think that there would be another day when we could be together, telling each other stories like that. I could think of any number of stories, but I really didn't expect that there would ever be a chance of that happening.

But then, Mac and Molly came back. They had their heads together for quite a while, and Mac had a serious look on his face, when he sat down next to me, and Molly sat down next to jill. "We

238

have been talking it over, and these girls are really wanting to get out of here. The bus does not come until next week, so I was thinking we might offer them a ride."

"That's right," Molly said, "we have enough tip money, so we could pay for the gas, and Jill could cook some extra bread in the morning before we hand in our resignation. We might have to work until three, but the boss knows plenty of those farm girls that are looking for work, so I don't think there would be any problem."

I looked at Jill, and she was nodding her head in agreement, so what could I say? I stammered around a bit, "I think we were headed for the Rocky Mountains." "That's great. I always wanted to see the mountains. How about you, Jill?

"Oh, yes, when I lived in the swamp, I had a book once that had pictures of those mountains. I always wanted to see one for real." Just like that, the die was cast. Mac and I would wait around until three the next afternoon, then those girls would get in the car, and we would be off on a Rocky Mountain adventure. I could hardly wait.

Chapter 25

It was a long day for us, as we waited for the girls to get off work. Mac had a book to read, and I was working on my journal, trying to figure out how to put into words the miraculous thing that had happened, as I had met and talked to the girl of my dreams.

In the back of my mind, however, was the nagging suspicion that those girls would most likely want to go to the big city, where they could find shopping and excitement. That was definitely not my thing, and I had a deep fear that a day would come soon when I would see her no more.

We went to that café, of course, for breakfast and lunch, but what Molly said was true. The food was not very good, except for the biscuits Jill cooked for breakfast, and the pie for lunch.

They did get off at three, but they had to go to some little room they shared, and get their stuff, so it was almost four when they showed up at the park. Jill was carrying a paper bag of food, and what appeared to be a blue tablecloth with all her belongings wrapped up in it.

Molly had a quilt full of clothes and a bundle of stuff that appeared to be their bedding. Mac just opened the back hatch of the Jeep and stuffed it all inside, behind the back seat, and the girls got in the back seat.

Mac took the first shift, driving, while I was supposed to be the navigator, with my road atlas in my lap. Finding our way out of this place and back to the main highway turned out to be a real challenge, a puzzle of back roads. Mac and Molly had a running commentary of sorts, but Jill just rode along, staring out the window. I was hoping that she was happy to be on the road, but maybe she was worried about how she was going to survive out in the world. Maybe, I thought, she is planning a big shopping trip.

It just goes to show that I did not have a clue how the female mind works, for I had not been close to any of them since I was a kid. I started out on a farm, a bit isolated, and I had no sisters to learn from.

It was along towards evening by the time we found the main highway. The Road Atlas showed a long, mostly straight line from there to Colorado, which was the nearest we could get to the mountains. Too far for one day's drive, though.

It was dark when we came to the first town of any size. There was one motel, and Mac checked at the desk. All they had available was two rooms with two double beds in each one. Everyone was agreeable, so he got us lined up. Jill and Molly in one room, and me and Mac in the other.

We had been snacking on the leftover rolls and food that Jill had brought with us, so there was no reason to go out to dinner. I guess what I am saying was that I never really got a chance to talk to Jill that day, as much as I wanted to.

We slept in, so it was not a very early start the next morning. It was my turn to drive, so I had to watch the road. Everyone seemed to be very quiet this morning, as they all seemed to be lost in their own thoughts, probably worried about where they might end up. At least it was a companionable silence.

We were crossing the longest, straightest, and most barren area of the entire trip, when Jill said, "I think I see the top of a mountain ahead." I didn't see anything, but most of my attention was on the road.

Finally, about noon, we came to a junction with another road. There was a paved area, just before the stop, probably provided for people that needed to stop and rest their eyes.

I got out to stretch my legs, and when I walked up to the highest point, I could see, not one, but the tops of two peaks. Of course, the girls did the same and they were quite excited for it was their first view of the mountains, even though they were far away at this point. It was Mac's turn to drive, so I got back in the passenger seat, and began to study the road map for this area.

There were a couple of choices at this point, so I tried to explain, as I did not want to be the one to pick a route.

"First, we could turn right and just over Raton Pass, we would come to Trinidad, which appears on the map to be a good-sized town, with lots of hotels and restaurants."

"And people and traffic," said Molly. "Well, if we take that road, it leads to Denver, which has over a million people."

Jill spoke up "We sure don't want to go there."

Now, I was surprised as this was not what I expected at all.

"What if we turned left?"

"That's a long road, but it leads to Albuquerque, which is also a million people" Now, it seemed that everyone was groaning with disappointment, so I looked at the map again.

"Okay, if we turn left for a short way, there is a road heading west, that seems to go more in the direction of those mountains we can see" I showed them on the map, and they were all in agreement. "We want to see mountains, not people." It was Mac's turn to drive, so I was looking at the map.

He took the left turn onto a major highway, but we only drove a few miles when we saw a sign that pointed to the right.

Just a small sign, with a couple of names on it. I think it said Cimmaron, 50 miles, and Taos 250 miles, something like that.

Now, this road was a big disappointment, not because it was a bad road, but because of the scenery. This was just almost barren desert, with an occasional cactus or dead tree. We passed one building, which seemed to be some sort of bar or watering hole. We could not imagine that there would be anyone living out there to even come in for a beer. I did not see how a cow could survive out there, it if had twenty acres to pick from.

Despite that, Mac kept on driving, and gradually, we could see on the right, the greenery of a forest. The further we drove, the bigger the forest became, until that was all you could see in that direction, just miles and miles of green forest. Suddenly, as we topped a rise, there was a break in the trees, and we could see two mountains in the distance. I checked the map. They were marked. "That is the Spanish Peaks. They are the highest mountains in this area."

It was such a beautiful sight, and the girls were so

thrilled by it, that we stopped right there, and finished off what was left of the food that the girls had brought with them. Jill was just beaming. "Oh, this is so exciting. The mountains and the green trees. So different from the swamp, where I used to live."

I could understand the feeling. After two years in the desert. This was like a revelation, of sorts. I made a silent vow, right then, that if Jill liked this kind of scenery so much, I would do whatever it took to help her find a place like this to settle.

It was my turn to drive, and as we went along, we began to enter the forest, just patches here and there at first, and then thicker, until there was nothing to see but green out of either window, now, it was mostly pine forest. We seemed to be gaining elevation, and we came out into a big open area, surrounded by forest. There was some sort of a rest stop here, a single building by itself, just shaded by a single group of trees.

It appeared to be a facility provided by the highway department, and it had not only a rest room, but an information center. Reading the various travel guides, I learned that this area was the starting point for several bike trails that led from there in every direction, through field and forest. I also learned that we were in New Mexico, but very close to the border with Colorado. This was apparently the place on the sign that was fifty miles from the main highway, and still another 200 miles to Taos.

I was still in the driver's seat, and we drove into more forest. There were occasionally some little side roads to parking lots, where the weekend bikers could take to the trails. As the afternoon wore on, there were less and less side roads, and more and thicker trees, a mixture of pines and deciduous trees, in all shades of green.

Still, Jill said nothing, but I could glance up in my rear-view mirror once in a while and see her watching it all out the window with a pleased expression on her face.

It was late afternoon when I happened to notice a little side road to the right. It was paved, but narrow and with no yellow stripe down the middle. There was no indication of a town, and I probably would not have taken that road, except that I saw a sign beside the road, some distance away.

On an impulse I turned there; no one seemed to object so I drove about a half mile up to that sign. It was a very nice sign and it said, **Welcome to Colorful Colorado.** I heard a little cheer from the back seat, so I kept driving. We seemed to be in some sort of flat valley between the forests, which were green and bright in the late afternoon sun. the floor of the valley was flat, and it looked more like a hay field than a pasture. At any rate, I didn't see any animals grazing.

As we went along the valley seemed to be narrowing, while we seemed to be climbing in elevation.

Looking ahead of us, I could see the top of a mountain peak, so I kept on driving.

Another couple miles and the valley was becoming quite narrow, and then there was the first indication of a town. No sign or anything. The road sort of leveled off, and there was a cabin on the left. A very nice cabin, with a fenced area at the back. Then a couple more cabins, with the same sort of fence, a head high fence with woven wire.

"I know what those fences are for." offered Molly, "That's to keep the deer out of the garden." That got Jill's attention. "Really, you think we might see a deer?"

I was driving quite slowly now. It was such a beautiful area. Suddenly it came as a surprise that there was a town here. No sign or anything to announce it. There was a very nice large cabin made of logs, with three smaller cabins in a row next to it and a little sign that said, **'Cabins for rent'**

A little further along, we entered the main street of the town. There were stores on the right, with a couple cars parked in front.

There was a grocery store, a hardware store and a store with a sign that said, **General Merchandise.** "It looks like they have it all covered right there" said Mac, "Everything you might need, all in a row."

That was it, we came to the end of town. The little road continued, but there was a wide spot paved, and it appeared to be the normal thing to make a U-turn here, so I did.

Coming back down the street, on the right there was a long block of buildings, which appeared to be small offices and businesses. Some had little signs in the windows, I saw one with various signs, and Jill spoke up "Look, sewing notions"

Another one said something like 'Real estate and Insurance. There were some that might have been empty. I could not tell because the late afternoon sun was coming over the top of the buildings and hitting me in the eye.

However, one of the signs said **Café** and that got everyone's attention. Mac, of course, was always thinking ahead. "Maybe we should get a place to stay for tonight, then we could get cleaned up and go have a nice dinner."

Molly agreed quickly, "That sounds like fun" and Jill said, "Yes, this is the nicest little town I have ever seen."

There was no hotel or motel, so we drove back down to the place where the sign said **Cabins for rent**. Mac and I went into the main cabin, and a nice-looking, middle-aged lady came out of the back room, and greeted us at a counter, just like you would expect in a fine hotel. Mac enquired about a room for the night.

"Certainly. Do you have any idea how long you might be staying?"

"No, we were just passing through, and decided to stop for supper. No idea how long we might stay."

"Well, it doesn't matter. It's just that it is less if you rent by the week. Otherwise, it is fifty dollars a night, per cabin."

I paid for one and Mac paid for the other, and she handed us two keys. We went back out to the car, and I handed one key to Jill while Mac opened the back of the Jeep and got out whatever clothes and stuff we might need.

Each cabin was the same, two small bedrooms, a kitchenette, and a bathroom with a combination shower – tub.

We agreed to meet in an hour, and we would go to supper at the café.

Mac and I took turns with the shower, and shaved and put on our best clothes, which really weren't much. "You know" Mac said, "If we were to keep doing this, we might have to find a clothing store and buy some better outfits. I don't have anything that would be nice enough to dance in, do you?" I agreed. I had a new pair of blue jeans.

That would work for supper, but not for a dance. "Probably no place to dance around here, anyway."

The sun was almost gone by the time we met outside the cabins. It felt good, especially since those gals looked sharp. Nothing fancy, but they had their hair fixed. I don't think Jill ever used makeup, but to me, she was the picture of poise, like a model in a magazine. We agreed that there was no need to drive. It was just a nice evening walk.

As we went along, the girls were admiring every little thing. There were wildflowers growing in the hayfield next to the road. No sidewalk here, but also no traffic, so we just walked down the middle of the highway.

We passed one of those cabins with the high fence around the back yard. From where we were, it was hard to tell, but it appeared that there were all kinds of foliage growing there. "Probably got carrots and radishes," one said, and the other said, Maybe tomatoes and beets" That didn't thrill me much as I never liked beets.

All too soon, it seemed like we came to the edge of town, where a sidewalk began in front of the little shops along the left side of the street. Now the girls were window shopping. There was a lot of "Look at that" and "What could you use that for?"

Now, I was just hungry, so I was quite happy to hold the door open for everyone to enter the café.' Inside it was cool and dim but with a homey feeling. Little Knick knacks adorned the walls, and a couple old plates on shelves. There was a choice of tables or booths, and Molly picked a table, sort of in the middle of it all.

A very nice-looking young lady came out of the kitchen to wait on us. She brought everyone a menu and a glass of water without being asked. It was no trouble for me. I saw the words, "Country fried steak, served with potatoes and gravy."

The others ordered various things from soup to salad to a T-Bone steak for Mac. In a short time, we were all busy, eating everything and agreeing that it was delicious. "I wish we would have had food like this in that last place we worked." Jill agreed. "This is almost as good as Juliet' and she added "This is nicer, because there is no traffic noise from the highway."

As we all were having dessert, Mac commented on that to the waitress. Naturally, he struck up a conversation, as he always did. "There does not seem to be many people around this evening."

"Well, no, not many come into town in the middle of the week, but if you come here on the weekend, you would be surprised. You might have trouble finding a parking space." "Hard to believe. What in the world would bring that many people into town?"

She pointed at the rear of the café. There was a big archway there and inside, there was only one dim bulb lighting the area. All you could see was a section of a highly polished floor.

"We have a group of local guys that have put together a band. They come in and play for us on Friday and Saturday nights. Better come early, because by nine o'clock, you won't get a table, or a parking place, and by ten you will be lucky to get on the dance floor."

I saw Mac looking at Molly. She was smiling, and Jill was smiling, and I knew right then, that we were going to be here longer than one day.

Chapter 26 ══════════════════════════════════

Not so early, the next morning we gathered again in front of the cabins, to go to breakfast. We had all slept in, as the beds were soft, and the quiet and the altitude combined to give us a sense of well-being; a feeling that life should be enjoyed at a slower rate.

As we walked up the highway, we were noticing different things, like birds; a meadowlark sang his little tune out in the meadow, and little yellow butterflies floated past. Every little thing seemed to be a new enjoyable experience for Molly and Jill.

When we reached the sidewalk, we turned and looked back. You could see two different mountain peaks in two different directions, and it seemed to be a high point of the day. At least a good way to start, as far as Jill and Molly were concerned.

In the café, a different, and very nice looking young girl waited on us. Once again, we all chose our favorite things from the menu. I had a plateful of big pancakes, with hash browns and ham and lots of syrup.

When we finished eating, the girls excused themselves, saying they needed the powder room. That left me with Mac, and he told me that he had already gone to the main cabin and paid the lady for two more days. "We have to stay, at least until dance night"

I had no argument for that, and when the girls came back, he and Molly headed out the door, he to check out the hardware store and she to check out the General Merchandise.

Now, I was alone with Jill, which I had been hoping for, at least for a couple of days. Strangely enough, I did not know quite what to say. She smiled and said, "I met a lady in the powder room, and she talked to me. Everyone here seems to be so nice. After the way they treated us in that last place we worked, this place seems like a dream." "Well, I guess we are going to stay here for at least a couple more days. It seems that Molly and Mac have made up their minds to waltz. Do you know how to polka?" "No, I don't, but I am a quick learner.

I'm sure you can teach me." This boosted my spirits a notch, as I had almost been afraid to ask her to go to the dance with me.

"I would like to take you to the dance, but I might have to get some new clothes before then. I'm not sure my blue jeans are the proper wear for it." "Me, too" she said, "All my clothes are old and worn out."

I got out my wallet and pulled out some bills, placing them on the table in front of her. That got an immediate reaction. "Chris, you don't need to give me money." "Don't worry about it It's like a loan, remember? We will settle up, eventually."

She still looked unsettled, and a thought came into my head. "Jill, did you write to Global and tell them your location?"

"Yes, I did exactly what you said, I wrote to them and told them I was working in Juliet. They sent word back that, when there were any royalties, they would be placed into a bank account somewhere." "Then what happened?" "The tornado happened, and I lost the card with the address, I figured it didn't amount to anything anyway."

"But jill, your swamp turned out to be a major find in the oil business. They are still drilling wells on your land, and I must tell you that somewhere there is an account with your name on it. You could be a very rich woman."

I thought she would be happy, but she was not. She looked upset. "But I don't want to be rich. Grandpa warned me about rich people. They never seem to have enough, and they will stop at nothing to get it. I just want to have a roof over my head and a chance to be happy."

I realized I had to do something quick, to calm her down. "That's okay. I will check it out for you, and if there is any money, you can have it put into a trust for your descendants, okay?" That seemed to calm her down, so I said, "Look, all we need to think about is the next couple of days, so just take this money and go shopping. Get yourself a new dress, or whatever it takes to go to a dance, okay?"

That seemed to help her decide, and she picked up the money, reminding me that it was just a loan. She left, and I sat there a while, drinking my coffee, and considering my options. There were certain things I had to know before I could plan my course of action. I walked down the sidewalk to where I thought I had glimpsed a post office. Sure enough, there it was, with U.S. Postal Service painted in red and blue letters at the bottom of the front window. There was another nice-looking middleaged lady behind the counter. I was beginning to think that this town had some kind of a production center that stamped out nice middle-aged ladies and very nice-looking young waitresses.

She said, as I expected, "What can I do to be of assistance today?" "I was thinking that I might need to contact someone in Denver for information. Should I airmail, or is there a telegraph office?" "Oh, no, we don't have anything like that." she pointed and there was a phone on the counter against the other wall, with a little sign saying, "For the use of customers" "There will probably be some charges, as I might tie up the phone for a while."

"No problem. They will notify me of any charges, and you can pay me later."

Okay, I was beginning to think that this town must have some kind of law requiring everyone to be nice to strangers I got the Global card out of my pocket, with the list of office numbers on the back, and dialed the financial office, hoping that Fritz was still there, as I had met him a time or two when I checked in to pick up my paycheck.

"Good morning, this is Fritz." "Morning Fritz. This is Chris Jensen." In my ear I heard a burst of laughter. "What's so funny, Fritz?"

"You are one of those poor souls, whose name was in the pot when the boss decided to send somebody off to the far side of the world."

He was laughing harder now, just thinking about it. "You guys drew the short straw and I always wondered what happened to you. I figured you probably got drowned in a sand dune or kicked by a camel or something."

He was so cheerful about it, that he had me laughing, too, a little bit.

"Well, despite the bosses' intentions, I somehow managed to survive, and after two years, I managed to dig my way out." I looked over at the lady behind the counter. She was trying her best not to hear, but it was such a small room, there was no way she could help but overhear the conversation. She probably was thinking I dug my way out of prison.

"Look, Fritz, I served my time in the desert, but now they have shipped me back to the States, and I need some information, if I can still call in a favor."

His laughter settled down to a chuckle. "Sure, Chris, whatever you need, just name it."

"Okay, I need two current financial statements, one for me and one for Jill Johannsen. Maybe I don't have that last name quite right, but she is a landowner, and her account should show royalties paid in."

"All right. Yours is no problem, but hers might take a little longer."

I hung there on the phone for a while. I smiled at the nice lady, and she smiled back. "We just stopped in for supper the other night. And decided to stay a few days longer" She smiled and replied. "You are probably the folks staying down in the cabins."

"That's right, and we have been eating in the café. It's a nice town and has good food. We really like it here." She made no comment, and Fritz came back on the line. He had a different tone to his voice now, and he wasn't laughing anymore.

"It looks like you did pretty well on that assignment to Africa. Very well indeed, but then not as well as the lady with the oil wells. Oh, my."

"Look, Fritz, we don't want to discuss figures over the phone. Is there any way you can get those figures to me?" I looked at the lady, and she pointed to a fax machine. Fritz said he could fax them, and she gave me the code which I relayed to him. In a few minutes, the machine spit out two sheets of paper. Long sheets with lots of figures on them.

The lady tore off the two sheets without looking at

them. She handed them to me, and I asked her how much I owed for the service and the call.

"I won't know for a while. All those charges show up on my reports at the end of the day. You can check with me tomorrow."

I laid a twenty on the counter "Just in case I don't get back" and went out the door with the figures in my hand.

Now, this was the type of little town that had some benches along the sidewalk for people to rest on, if their feet got tired, so I sat down on one and studied the figures. It took a while to soak in. with back pay and bonuses for all those years, I had 127, o00 dollars in my account, and Jill had 5i7, 000 in hers.

The difference was that my active earning life was, you might say, at an end, while hers was still increasing exponentially.

How was I going to explain this to a lady who would no doubt be a millionaire in a couple years? I decided it was best not to tell her any exact amounts. I had best explain to her that she had plenty of money, if she needed anything, or if she wanted to pay me back. I didn't need the money either, but it boiled down to whatever would make her happy. It just pleased me to know that she would never want for anything again, knowing just a little about the frugal life she had spent with her grandpa. As I rose from the park bench, I happened to glance in the window next door. It was the office that said Insurance and Real Estate. There were some little posters in the window, advertising homes and acreages for rent or sale. Two of the posters were just alike, which caught my attention.

On a whim, I went inside. It was a very small office, with a desk, a couple of filing cabinets, a couple of chairs and a table on the far wall, with some brochures for those who wished more information.

The man's name was Roy, and I quickly decided that he must be married to one of the nice ladies in town, because he pushed all his work aside just to help me. In a soft voice, with a touch of a southern drawl, he asked me if there was anything he could help me with.

I introduced myself and proceeded to explain how the four of us happened to come into town. "It was just a whim, but it turned out well, as we all like it here." "Yes, well, we don't get many visitors here. We don't put out a sign or anything because most of the people here like peace and quiet. Most of us have come here over the years because we were trying to get away from city life. I know my wife and I did."

"But there must be tourists on that highway that goes west from here." "There is, but most of them are headed for a resort area about fifty miles west of here, a real tourist trap.

They even have a little ski area called Angel Fire." I began to get the picture. "No tourists, no traffic, no noise to mar the peace and quiet."

"That's right. Of course, we get a few that stray in once in a while, like for instance, the four in your party, but everyone says that you are all pretty peaceable."

That caught me by surprise, but it was just another lesson on the way the grapevine works in a small town. "You folks wouldn't mind, then, if we decided to stay a while."

"Not at all, as long as you don't get in any fights on Saturday night. That is usually the only time we need a Sheriff, if some of the boys get to mixing it up after the dance"

This seemed to be a word of warning as well as a word of advice, but I thought that it sounded like a good thing. That was what seemed to attract us here, was the peace and quiet.

"So, what have you done to keep it so peaceful?"

"We set up a sort of neighborhood watch. If someone put up a sign down on the highway, we would have someone there in a few minutes, taking it down.

If anyone happened to get past, we had people watching, and if they stopped to ask directions, they told them some big story about how they were on the wrong road, and the one they wanted was over east where those bike trails are.

Then, if they happened to get all the way through town, we put a little chain across the road just past the turnaround that said, 'Road closed due to mudslides' which was not that much of a lie because we had a big rain once and it really happened."

I thought about that for a few minutes. "But now, you have those two cottages for rent?"." "Yes, we do. It doesn't happen often, as there are very seldom ant empty houses in Pleasant Valley"

"I am assuming that you could show those to us, as a group, that is." "Certainly, just let me know when yo folks are ready to take a look."

"So, I have to ask, why tell me about it? You could

show those to anybody." "Yes, but we have already checked you out.

The lady next door said you worked for Global, and I already called them while you were sitting out front. Besides my wife said she thought you were okay. She really likes those two gals."

"Wait a minute. You must be married to the lady that runs the cabins." "You are correct, and I must tell you that nothing hardly ever gets by her. She has her eye on every car that comes into town."

We also had another thirty-minute discussion of different houses or plots of land that were for sale or rent.

Just things that might come in handy to know, if we should all decide to stay in this area.

Thinking back on that day, it's strange how a conversation like that could change your whole life. Strange but true.

Chapter 27

I went looking for Mac, and found him sitting on one of those little benches in front of the hardware store. He had a serious look on his face when he said, "I am beginning to think that the people of this town are all suffering from a case of terminal nice."

"Does that bother you a lot?"

"Not really. It's just an observation. Why do you ask?"

"Because we have been given an invitation to join the club."

"What are you talking about? What club?" "The club of nice people that live here, stay here, and work here, with a single goal; the goal of being nice, whatever the cost."

"You have to be kidding me, Buddy. Did you fall and hit your head? Maybe you have a concussion. We could go look for a hospital." "Nope. I'm fine, but we need to go for a ride. I will explain on the way."

As we started down the sidewalk, I asked him, "Where are the girls?" "I'm not sure. There was some mention of a sewing lesson at the notions store. I think they are learning how to stitch a pillowcase or something. It involved a pattern of some sort."

"Just as I figured. They are being inducted into the club."

"There's that club again. Are you wacked? Been into the sauce while I wasn't looking?" "Nope, none of the above. I suppose you gave Molly some money."

"Sure, everything I had on me. Why?"

"I did the same for Jill. I think we just paid their initiation fee into the club."

"Honestly, Buddy, if you don't quit with this club thing, I am going to get you admitted to the home for the criminally insane."

Of course, I liked to get Mac talking like that. it was fun to get him riled up, but I told him to get in the Jeep and I would give him the whole story on the way. I told him how they checked out everyone that came into town. "You need to understand that not everyone gets an offer to stay, and it's mostly because the lady that runs the cabins likes Jill and Molly. It's not because they like us, especially, but they are willing to put up with us, as long as we don't pick a fight with the cowboys on Saturday night."

"That shouldn't be too hard. I am really a very peaceable guy."

"Yeah, I know that, and you know that, but they

don't know that. they are depending on those girls to keep us under control"

Anyway, I told him about the financial statements, and the fact that Jill already had more money in the bank than we would ever see in our lifetime, and I cautioned him not to mention it to Molly. "Jill gets all upset at the very hint that she might be rich, so I will do everything in my power to keep her calm."

I figured I had him thoroughly briefed on the situation, so I turned my attention to the scene before us. We were driving on this little narrow, one lane road, and the valley was becoming narrower, with thick forest beginning to close in on both sides. There was so much green here, all shades of green the trees and the grass, that it was sort of overpowering.

In addition, we were rapidly gaining elevation. It was only about ten miles, but it felt like we were heading for the top of the world.

The further we went, the narrower the valley became and the thicker the trees.

So, when we came out of the trees into an open area, a clearing in the middle of it all, it was sort of like a curtain opened. The sun came shining in, and we stopped, and there were, in the background, stands of aspen trees that were beginning to turn color, just a hint of yellow showing through the green, a hint of what would soon come, as Autumn would be here before very long.

Mac shut the motor off, saying, "Whoa, Nellie, did I just pass out and wake up in a technicolor movie somewhere?"

"It is kind of nice, isn't it?"

We shut the motor off and got and walked around for a bit. The air was clear and quiet. The flashes of sunlight coming through the leaves of the aspen trees gave a peaceful feeling.

It was the kind of place where a guy could build a

little cabin with a little front porch, where he could set out in his rocker in the sun, just letting the day go by. A place to forget all your worries for a while. "How did you know about this place?" "I was talking with the Real estate man, and he mentioned it"

Mac seemed to be interested. "I suppose they want a high price for a location like this?"

I told Mac the price that Roy said we might be able to purchase it for.

"I don't know a lot about Real Estate, but I am certain sure that 40 acres has to be a bargain at this price."

"Roy told me that the price had been reduced a couple times, and it was a real bargain. I'm finding it hard to believe, myself."

We walked around the clearing one more time and talked it over. We agreed that it would be ideal for two cabins.

Finally, we got in the car and headed back to town.

It was my turn to drive, and we were both lost in thought as we drove back down that little road int town.

You know the funny thing is, here I am, actually considering buying a place to build a house and I don't even know the name of the town."

That was the first question I asked Roy, after we parked in front of the Real Estate office. "Well," he said in that soft southern drawl. "It seems that the first name of the settlement was Eureka, because some prospector found some gold back in the hills.

Then the name was changed to Swenson, when some men came here to work her for him, but then, they had some other words for him when it turned out to be a shallow vein, which quickly petered out.

Anyway, after a few years some of us came here, and began to tear down some of the old miners' shacks and replace them with homes. When we had a meeting to pick a name. one of the ladies suggested we call it Pleasant Valley, and it stuck, in spite of the fact that it's not a town name, more of a location."

Now, this was my first indication that Mac was thinking about actually buying some land and staying here. I didn't know quite how to take that idea, but I decided to keep my mouth shut and see what happened.

Roy got on the phone to the main office in Denver, talked a few minutes and when he hung up, he said. "Yes, those two parcels are listed for sale, pretty much at the price the developer paid for them."

"So, what would the total be, if we bought the whole thing, half for me and half for Chris?" "That would be about 30,000 for each of you."

Mac looked at me, "You think we can cover that?"

I gave him a thumbs up and he said, "Okay, I think we have a deal. When can we have the closing?"

"I can get the papers faxed from the office in Denver

and probably get everything ready in about two days. All I need is some confirmation that you have either the money or the financing necessary."

"No problem" I said, and I handed him my financial statement and he looked it over while I went next door to the post office and called Fritz. I was back in about ten minutes with Mac's financial statement, and there was already a paper on the desk for each of us to sign.

I walked out of there in a daze. "What did we just do? I never thought I would ever buy a piece of ground, just like that."

"Listen, Buddy" Mac said, "that was just too good of a deal to pass up. If we should decide to go elsewhere, we could list that place for sale and make a profit."

I thought about it for a minute. "I agree." "The thing is" he said, "Let's not tell the girls about this until after we go to the dance the next couple of nights.

Then we can sit down and decide if we want to sell or stay."

I didn't know if they would laugh the whole thing off. I would just have to be patient and see what would happen.

Hardest thing I ever had to do.

Chapter 28

It was beginning to feel so natural, having the girls next door. I was beginning to feel like, in one instant, that it could just go on forever, and then, in the next instant, dreading the reality that it could all come to an end at any moment. We had, each of us, spent some time in the General Mercantile that day, either in the men's clothing section, or the ladies.

So, I was outfitted with a new pair of brown slacks and a tan shirt. I might have even gone for a tie, but my feeling was that I might be overdressed at a country dance. I even had a pair of shiny new shoes, with leather soles, since my old boots most likely would not slide well on the dance floor.

Mac had a new outfit as well, and we waited out-side with a feeling of apprehension, as we both felt that this evening might well determine the path of our future life.

It was not quite dark yet when the girls came out. With a new red dress that complimented her dark hair, Molly was ready, and Mac was quick to take her arm and start up the hill.

Jill had a new cream-colored dress that seemed to suit her perfectly, and I hardly knew what to say. I smiled and she smiled, and I took her hand, and we took the evening walk.

There were already some cars parked on Main Street, and we had taken the waitress's words seriously that we should get there early if we wanted a table.

We chose a table for four in the corner nearest to the dance hall entrance. A nice young waitress ap-peared and informed us that if we did want to keep that table for the evening, we would need two things: the reserved sign on the table and four drinks visible.

I don't know what Mac and Molly ordered, but Jill and I, neither one wanted an alcoholic beverage, so I ended up with something called a Rob Roy, and she had a Shirley Temple. Both drinks would be emptied and refilled several times during the evening.

We didn't have much to say, while we waited for the music to begin. She seemed to be content just watching the people coming in, and the place was filling up fast. I just wanted to sit there and look at her. She was so gorgeous, with her hair fixed and her fingernails done. She used very little makeup, if any. She simply didn't need it. When we heard the band warming up, we went into the dance hall, which was decorated in a country sort of way. The music was a little bit country, too. They didn't play any polkas, but we watched the first dancers. They were doing some sort of a country two-step, and once we saw how it was done, we got out on the floor and gave it a try.

We might have stepped on each other's toes a couple of times, but by the third dance we had it down, and we were going around the floor just like old pros. We danced every dance until intermission when we sat down at our table.

Mac and Molly, I could see, were making the rounds, getting acquainted with everyone, as he liked to do.

A young cowboy came over and took a seat at our table. It seemed he wanted somebody to talk to, and he was telling us that he worked for a ranch that ran cattle out in the forest to the east of Pleasant Valley.

"This is the best place I ever worked." He said, "If you go to the ranches to the north, in the higher elevations, you get ice and snow, and if you go to the ranches to the south, in New Mexico, you have to contend with cactus and hot and dry.'

His name was Dale Thomas, and I thought he would have made an excellent advertisement for the area. I could see that he was really wanting to dance with Jill, and he asked her when the music started playing again, but as soon as that set was over, she came right back again, and we danced the rest of the night away. All too soon, it seemed, midnight rolled around and as they played the last dance, a slow one, I had a tight hold on her waist, and she was resting her head on my shoulder as we danced cheek to cheek.

It was a balmy late summer evening, as we walked back down the hill, talking about how much fun we had, and we both agreed that we could hardly wait to do it again. As we were saying goodnight, I managed to steal a little kiss on the front porch, and I was a happy guy as I anticipated the possibilities of days to come.

Chapter 29

Pleasant Valley was feeling more and more like home now, as I spent much of the day checking out the stores and sitting on the bench in front of the Real Estate office.

Most everybody came by here, every day, as the Post Office was next door, and there was no home delivery, so it was a great place to get acquainted.

By evening, I had at least a nodding acquaintance with most of the residents, so when we went to the dance on Saturday night, there were greetings all around.

The street was already packed with cars when we got there, and it was only because the waitress put a reserved sign on the table, that we even got one. The place was packed, and the band was warming up. We ordered drinks, as before, but they barely hit the table before Mac and Molly were off and running. It seemed that they already had a friendly acquaintance with every single person in the whole county, not just the town. We sipped our drinks in companionable silence until the music began and Jill and I took to the dance floor. We were starting to get the hang of the waltz, which they played about every fifth tune, and it was quickly becoming our favorite.

Of course, Mac and Molly were very accomplished at the waltz, and every time they twirled by, we were watching and trying to imitate their moves.

We only sat down at the table to sip our drinks when the band took an intermission break. It was like we were lost in our own little world, so we didn't talk to anyone, and we never danced with anyone else.

It was with a sense of anticipation that I walked

Jill back to the motel after the dance. I was the happy recipient of several kisses on the front porch, and we parted with the understanding that this was our last night at the motel. We both agreed that we wanted to stay here, and some more permanent lodgings were called for.

The next morning, being Sunday, the lady that ran the hotel pointed out to us that there was a path from the back door that would take us to the residential area of town that was behind the stores of the commercial area.

I had not previously been there, and I was so surprised to see an area the was so well planned with houses arranged around blocks, and with street signs and green lawns.

There was a park at one end of the area and the church at the other end. We, the four of us, took a seat in the back pew. It was a friendly church, with a lot of hymns singing, and a message from the pastor, about friendship and helping others. A very good way to spend the morning.

In the afternoon there was a picnic in the park. We were seated at a picnic bench, that is, three of us were seated. As usual, Mac was off somewhere greeting people and making contacts. I was seeking more contact with Jill in an effort to understand which way she was inclined to go.

"So, Jill, you understand that you have money, but you don't want to use it." "That's right. It's hard to explain but my grandpa taught me that it was only what I earned with my two hands that counted in life." Molly joined in. "I agree with that. we are both looking for jobs so we can stay here in Pleasant Valley."

"Well, Mac and I go along with that. We both want to stay here, but we can't stay in that motel forever. We would need a house to live in while we looked for a job."

Molly was not enthusiastic. "But there are no empty houses in Pleasant Valley, as far as I know."

"Ys, there is. I checked it out. Do you see those two little white cottages over there, just at the edge of the trees?"

Both looked. "Don't tell me they are empty? They couldn't be, both of them?" "Sure, I see the Real Estate man over at the next table. Let me see if he will come over and tell you about it."

Roy was happy to do so. "Those houses both belong to an old lady by the name of Loretta, who had them built for her two kids when they got married and needed a place for them to raise their families. But now, they have all moved off to the big city, and Loretta has no other use for them, so she has enlisted me to rent them out for her. I have the keys, so I can show them to you now, If you like."

He was interrupted by the return of Mac. "What's going on?"

"Come on." Molly said, "We're going to look at a house."

Roy had the keys and unlocked both front doors, and we all trooped through the houses. They were both furnished; not fancy but quite serviceable, and soon it was agreed. Mac and I would rent one house and Moly and Jill, the other one.

We only had to walk back to the motel and collect what possessions we had there, put it all in the Jeep and drive up to where the entrance street was located, just past the General Store. I had not even noticed it before. It was like a hidden entrance to the residential area, with no street sign.

Of course, there were street signs there and we were at the intersection of Third and Pearl.

That evening, as we all sat on the picnic bench in our backyard, we all agreed that we had found a home. Now, all we needed to do was get a job.

Chapter 30

Life was good in Pleasant Valley, except for one thing. The problem with Jill and her understanding of the use of money. "I am really trying, Jill, to understand how you can have all this money" I showed her the financial statement that proved it. "Yet you refuse to use it to provide any part of your residential needs."

"No, I cannot do that. It goes against everything that my grandpa taught me. It only matters if I earn it myself, with my own two hands."

"Yet you say that you want no part of anything that I might build with money I have." I produced my financial statement, that also showed me to be financially solvent. "Even if I already own the ground on which to build a house for you to live in." "No, it only matters if we can both work together to produce something worthwhile." Now, I was bumfuzzled. I could not understand how we both could have a fortune in the bank and still not be able to do anything with it to produce something that we obviously both needed.

As usual, it was Mac that provided the answer. "Hey, I got a job."

He got a job with a lumber company, as the yard boss in charge of the loads of trees coming into the sawmill, and the loads of lumber going out to different locations.

Coming home from work one day, when we were all seated at the picnic table in the back yard, he announced to all of us. "I hear that a lot of our lumber is being used to build a new Forest Ranger office, to versee the new Park areas that are being opened up by the Forest Service in the next couple of months."

"I suppose they are taking applications for the new positions that need to be filled." Molly was excited.

"Sure, there are. How did you know that? There a number of openings. Maybe you guys should go apply." We all applied. The timing was excellent, as there were all kinds of job openings, and we had our applications in before anybody else.

Molly and Jill got the job of running the office, where they answered the phones and greeted the visitors, selling them permits and giving out maps of the trails. In short, they did just about everything including keeping the time sheets for the employees.

That included me, as I got the job of Trail guide, which I liked very much. It was sort of like being on my own the way I liked it, but without the heat and the loneliness of the desert.

The perk of the job was that I could stop in at the office once in a while and steal a kiss when nobody was looking.

"How about it, Jill, are we both making our own way now?"

"I guess we are."

"So, are you going to marry me now?" "Nope, not until the first of June."

"But, Jill, that is almost a whole month." "It doesn't matter. Grandpa said that anything worth having was worth waiting for."

The thing was, that Molly had adopted the same outlook as Jill, so Mac was also playing the waiting game.

"I never thought it would be so hard, having to wait for something. I have waited on ships; I have waited on planes. I even waited on you guys to find oil in the desert, but nothing was this hard to wait for."

I could only sympathize with him, but some thigs, like grandpa said, were worth waiting for.

It would be a double wedding, on June first, in the church of Pleasant Valley.

Mac and Molly would say "I do" first, and then we would switch places, and they would stand up for Jill and I as we said, "I do."

Life was good, in Pleasant Valley.